FIGHTING WORDS

A NOVEL

FIGHTING WORDS

Copyright © 2020 Taylor Danae Colbert

Published: Taylor Danae Colbert 2020

www.taylordanaecolbert.com

Editing: Jenn Lockwood Editing

Cover Design: Taylor Danae Colbert

ISBN: 9781679708657

For you, Dad, and all the other good guys.

P.S. Please don't actually read this book.

1

MARYN

I actually look pretty hot.

Keely did my hair, my blonde locks in these big, wispy waves down my back. I'm wearing one of her sequined halters—not one I would have purchased for myself, but I'm trying to be open-minded —black skinny jeans that almost required surgery to get on, and extra-high wedges. As far as I go, I'm looking pretty good.

I feel good, too. Exams are over. I graduate from Melladon University in less than a week. We're going out to the beach this weekend, and I happen to know that Shawn Jacobs has personally asked if I'm going to be there.

I already had a job interview over video chat and have scheduled a second one back in New York at one of the top PR agencies in Manhattan. My family is coming down for graduation, and it's just going to be an all-around great week. Starting with tonight. Shawn might be at the bar, and I'm ready for one last college fling. I need to get laid tonight.

"Ready, hoe?" Keely asks, bumping her hip into me to scoot me out of her way as she bends over the sink to re-apply mascara for the third time. I bump her back —I've got a lot more in the trunk than she does—to fluff my hair one more time and do a half-spin to double-check that my ass looks as good as I think it does.

"Ready, bitch," I say. She smiles. Her red hair is extra fiery tonight, and I'm always jealous of how perfectly straight she can make it. She's petite with almost no ass but double the chest you'd think someone of her stature would have.

I'm the exact opposite: fairly tall, awkwardly slender, with a decent-sized booty and absolutely nothing up front. We always joke that if someone slammed us together real hard, we'd make the "perfect" woman.

"We're picking Ellie up on the way," she says, and I nod, following her out of the bathroom. "Oh, then we are meeting Trey there. And Shawn," she adds, pinching my side. I swat her hand away and smile. "Don't forget your bag. We got a few hotel rooms, but I assume you'll end up in Shawn's."

I sigh quietly as we walk out the door and commence with my Shawn daydreaming. He's big, broad, and surfer-esque—just like a lot of the guys at Melladon—with shaggy blond hair and perfectly bronzed skin. He's the most comparable thing to a human Ken doll you've ever seen. And I've been in his bed. Multiple times.

College was way too fun for me. I ran away from Long Island as fast as my high school legs could carry me and got down here to Melladon, this perfect little school on the Gulf Coast of Florida. Sunshine, warm weather, and most importantly, not a soul from my hometown. That's the beauty of it.

But now, it's time to go back. And with no public relations job prospects down here in Florida, and quite a few in Manhattan, moving back north is my only option. But it's been five years. People forget. They move on.

At least, I hope they have. Because secretly, I don't think I have, and I don't need anyone else to join the party.

We pull up in front of Ellie's apartment building, and Keely calls her. Ellie promptly skips out of the apartment building she lives in on campus. She's been an RA all four years, and on-campus living never really grew old on her.

"Hey, Ell," Keely says.

"Hi, my boos," Ellie says, her sweet brown bob falling perfectly into place as she slides in. "Let's fucking do this!"

The two of them talk, go on about their exams, discuss plans for the beach, and figure out when their families are getting into town. I hear it all going down in the background, but my mind is still on New York. On home. On my family. Wondering if I'm going to move forward or jump right back into the nightmare that was my life five years ago.

"Yoohoo, Earth to Maryn," Keely says, waving her hand in my face as we park.

"Yeah, yeah, sorry," I say, unbuckling and hopping out. Ramsay's is a bar on the first floor of the Sandgate Hotel, a big, fancy hotel right on the beach, just a few minutes from campus. It's a Melladon tradition to spend the night before graduation at Ramsay's, and the hotel blocks a bunch of rooms for seniors to spend the night—

to promote safe drinking-and-driving practices. It's a far cry from the rundown, cheap-ass bars we went to our first few years. Going to Ramsay's is a rite of passage for Melladon seniors. It means you're stepping up in the real world. You know that money will be coming in soon. You're no longer in the same class as the rest of the student body. And baby, it's a wonderful feeling.

As we're getting out of the car, we hear whistling from across the parking lot. Trey rushes over to us, pushing himself up against Keely and squeezing her butt as he kisses her neck. She nuzzles back against him before spinning on her heel and kissing him way more passionately than necessary for a public parking lot.

Blech. They're so disgustingly adorable. They've been together since the third week of freshman year. We've sat with Keely and held her hand during their early-stage, bullshit fights, and we've been there when Trey asked Ellie and me to go ring shopping for her. They'll be engaged by the end of the year, and it's not hard to see that it's one of those meant-to-be kind of loves.

Ellie, on the other hand, is sort of a hot mess—in and out of different guys' beds, on and off all the hook-up apps. She's finally slowing down, but that's because she's found a longer-term catch. One I'm not particularly happy about.

"Professor Dickface meeting you here?" Keely asks as Trey swings an arm around her shoulders. We walk in through the hotel lobby and to the high-top table that Trey reserved for us weeks ago.

"It's Dick-*son*," Ellie says, rolling her eyes. "And no. He doesn't like to mingle with students until they are officially graduated."

I can't help but snort, and Keely stops in her tracks.

"So does fucking one of his students not count as mingling?" she asks. Ellie's jaw drops. She rolls her eyes again as she hangs her sweater up on the back of her chair.

"Fuck you, Keely," Ellie says, holding her hand up to wave over a waiter. She orders us each a round of shots to get the night rolling, then turns back to Keely to defend herself for the fiftieth time in two weeks. "He hasn't been happy in years. She tricked him into getting pregnant so he'd stay with her."

Keely snorts as she throws back her shot.

"He's a grown-ass man. And you're the woman wrecking his family," Keely says. Though I'm not as blunt with Ellie, Keely and I are one-hundred percent on the same page here. What Ellie's doing is wrong. She blames it on this undeniable attraction her and Professor Dickson share. She says the moment she walked by his office, they couldn't keep their eyes off each other.

The first time he asked her to stay after his class to review her grade, they had sex on his desk. And as she's sworn to us multiple times: "they couldn't stop themselves." When Keely and I rolled our eyes, she kept going.

"I'm serious. I couldn't stop my hands from touching him. It was like all my senses went numb. I needed him so badly, and that hasn't stopped," Ellie had told us in our apartment that night.

Keely has shared plenty of sex stories about her and Trey, too. Like how they just had to have sex in the middle of one of the campus parking lots in the back of his car in broad daylight one time. They couldn't wait the five-minute drive to one of their apartments.

Or how hard it was to hold off the one night they realized they didn't have a condom. More babbling bullshit that I cannot relate to.

Don't get me wrong, it's not that I haven't had sex. It's not that I haven't had *good* sex. Shawn is pretty good in that department. So are most of the other guys I've been with. But no dick has ever made me crazy enough to lose my goddamn mind. To risk getting arrested in a public place. To go against my morals.

No way. There's no such thing.

"You just haven't had the right dick," Keely said to me one night when we were discussing our latest sexcapades. I rolled my eyes.

"A dick like *that* does not exist. You two are just weak," I told them.

We've now been waiting for our onion rings and hot wings for twenty-five minutes, and the waiter hasn't been back to take our drink orders in a hot minute. Not that I don't like listening to my friend discuss the extramarital affair she's having with a man whose wife had a baby three weeks ago, but it's not high on my priority list.

"I'm gonna go get us some drinks," I say, excusing myself and hopping down off the pub chair.

"Excuse me," I say, leaning over the edge of the bar and trying to speak up so the bartender can hear me. This place has gotten increasingly more loud and more crowded since we sat down. "Excuse me," I say again, louder. A few people around me look over for a second before turning back to their evenings.

"You're gonna have to be louder than that, sweetheart," a man says. His voice is clean and smooth, like a piece of glass. I turn my head and see him. He's standing in the middle of a crowd of about ten guys and girls all mingling together. He seems huge, much taller than the other men he's with. His skin is dark under his light-green button-up that is stretching to curve itself around his chest and arms. He's got one hand in the pocket of his slacks, the other wrapped around a beer. And then our eyes meet.

I wouldn't forget those green eyes anywhere. They match his shirt perfectly, even standing out under the shitty bar lighting. The smile leaves his lips when he sees me, too.

My jaw drops, and my eyes narrow.

This fucking guy.

For five years, I've wanted nothing but to nut-punch him, drop-kick him in public, pop his tires, key his car. When I left for school, I thought I was leaving all this bullshit behind. I made it through four years without having to see or talk to anyone from home. I was the only one from my graduating class to come to Melladon, and I wanted to keep it that way.

But I'm not the first from home to ever attend.

Wyatt Mills, the bane of my existence, graduated before I got to high school. And he happens to be an alumnus of Melladon. But fortunately for him, he graduated before I even started here.

"Oh," he says when our eyes meet. I see his chest heaving up and down, but his eyes never drop from mine. And for some reason, that bugs me. He should grovel. He should be nervous, apprehensive, guilty.

But he's not. He's cocky, sure of himself. His eyes narrow on mine.

The bartender slides a drink down the bar, and before it reaches its rightful owner, I stick my hand out and grab it, ignoring the, "Hey, that's mine," coming from next to me. I take a few steps down the bar, headed right toward him.

This is it. This is the moment I've been waiting for. Five years.

This one's for my dad, motherfucker.

I step dangerously close to him, causing the crowd of beautiful alumni to separate slightly. I'm inches away from him now, and the scent of the cologne he's wearing would be enough to knock me out of my panties if I didn't want to bash his head in with a bat.

"Wyatt Mills," I say, taking a sip of the mystery drink in my hand without letting my glare waver. He swallows.

"Maryn," he says with a curt nod. "It's been a while."

I feel this weird, sadistic smile spread across my lips as I take one step closer to him. Then, I take what's left in the glass and turn it over upside down on his chest.

"Not long enough," I whisper before setting the glass down on the bar and walking away.

I get back to the table, and I'm shaking. I never pull off shit like that. And though I know I didn't look as calm, cool, and collected as I was picturing, the sound of his friends "ohhhing" as I walked away was enough to help me keep my shit together.

"You okay?" Trey asks. Keely and Ellie look up at me. I sit down at the table and grab an onion ring, my hand shaking as I shove it in my mouth.

"Yeah, I'm just, I..." I stammer in between bites.

"Jesus, Mare, you look like you've seen a ghost," Ellie says, patting my back. I let my eyes carefully trail back over to the bar where Wyatt and his crew were standing. And as our eyes meet again, I feel my body freeze.

"I wish. Unfortunately, he's very much alive," I say. Then I stand up. "I think I'm gonna go up to the room. I'm not feeling too hot."

They all stand up to protest, but I wave them off.

"Do you want us to walk you up?" Keely asks. I smile and shake my head.

"Thanks, but I think I can make it up a few floors in an elevator." They nod and hug me goodnight.

"Oh, Mare," Trey calls, "when Shawn gets here, do you want me to have him come to your room or..."

I sigh and shake my head.

"Not really feelin' it tonight," I say as I stalk off. And despite Shawn's Ken-like physique, that's the truth. Seeing your mortal enemy can have crushing effects on your libido.

I grab my bag and make my way to the front desk, giving them Trey's name. They give me the key to one of the rooms and point me to the elevator. As the doors open, I'm pleased to note that I'm the only one in it. But just as the doors are closing, a long, brown, slender hand pushes through the opening, making the doors slide back open.

And in steps Mr. Mills himself.

And suddenly, I feel sick all over again.

2

DECEMBER 2014 - MARYN

I'm not sure how much longer I can stare at this stupid study guide before my head explodes. I know I'm not getting college credit with this dumb AP exam, but my parents are paying for me to take it anyway since I "worked so hard" in the class all semester. It's the first official night of winter break, but I don't have much going on, so I'm spending it studying like the true nerd that I am.

But it's senior year. I've been working hard since I could hold a pencil. And now I'm halfway done with my last year of schooling before I'm off to college. I have my top-five list: NYU, Cornell, Boston University, Penn State, and my backup, this small school in Florida called Melladon. It's a good school and has a good communications program, but it's really far away. But it's just my backup.

Tomorrow is Christmas Eve, and I need these days off more than ever. Senioritis is definitely kicking in big time, and I need the mental break.

My phone rings on my bed as I get up off the floor to grab it. It's a text from Shelly.

Are you coming out tonight?

Coming where?

A bunch of us are meeting at Stone Creek Park to go sledding. I roll my eyes. It's as cold as a witch's tit outside, and we've already gotten two big snowstorms even though it's only December. My phone buzzes again.

Matt's coming.

My eyebrows shoot up. Matt has been on my radar for months now. He and Tanya Meadow supposedly went at it in the gym after a basketball game once, but that has never been proven true. He's the basketball MVP and rivals me for highest grade in all of our classes. He's a top prospect as far as I'm concerned.

I'll be there, I reply. I dress in as many layers as I can find while making myself not look too frumpy or stuffed. I need to be warm—but sexy.

I make my way downstairs and grab for my keys just as my dad is coming around the corner from the kitchen to the key rack.

"Where you off to, kid?" he asks.

"A bunch of us are meeting to sled," I say, pulling my beanie on.

"Love that you kids are still getting outside," he says. "Tell Shelly she still owes me her research paper from last week." I roll my eyes. Yes, my dad is a history teacher. At my school. Like, where my friends see him, and have to talk to him, and know that I'm his kid. But if I'm being honest, it doesn't bother me as much as it should bother a teenage girl. In fact, he's kind of the man. So, ipso facto, I'm kind of the man's daughter. It's got its perks.

"Will do," I say. "Where are you going?"

"Leave it to your mother to forget chicken when she offers to make chicken pot pie for Christmas Eve dinner," he says with a smile. I laugh.

"That's Mom for you," I say. He follows me out the door, and I say goodnight as he hops into his car, and I hop into mine.

An hour later, I'm sulking in the parking lot of the park while my friends are taking turns chugging beers and jumping onto each other like wild animals before taking off down the hill. Matt was a no-show, but now I'm stuck here because they are all drunk and need a ride home.

Their drunk asses are finally ready to go, and I drop the last of them off and pull into the driveway. I go inside quietly, hushing the dog before he wakes everyone up. But I hear the TV on in the living room.

"What are you doing up, Dad?" I ask him as he turns to greet me.

"Reruns of *M*A*S*H* are on. Couldn't pass that up," he says with a smile. I drop my stuff on the ground by the door and kick off my boots. I take off about twelve layers and skip over toward him, plopping down on the couch next to him. I love *M*A*S*H*, and I *love* watching it with my dad. It's our thing, just the two of us.

"Did you get the chicken?" I ask, picking around the remnants of his popcorn bowl.

"Yep. Saw Willa Mills up there while I was shopping," he says.

"Oh, cool," I say. Willa is a grade below me. She's the captain of the girls' volleyball team. We had P.E. together last year, but she tended to lead the pack on the mile runs while I tended to bring up the rear, so we didn't talk much.

"Ready for that test?" he asks me, sticking his hand back in the bowl to pull out some of the last pieces.

"Ugh, I don't know. I hate that I have to stress about it all break," I say.

"You don't. Don't stress about it. Take it head-on, kid," he says, not taking his eyes off the screen. I smile. Dad is so matter-of-fact. I'm a lot like my mom: anxious, Type A, a worrier. But Dad has a different mindset. He's a doer, not a worrier. My younger brother Tucker inherited that gene from him, and it's one I'm most envious of.

Tucker is three years younger than me and is sailing through his first year of high school. He's smart as a whip but puts in minimum effort and gets results that are irritatingly close to mine. But he's like Dad: matter-of-fact, to the point, and has way more common sense than should be allowed for one person.

THE NEXT MORNING is Christmas Eve, and—to be expected—Mom is running around like a chicken with her head cut off. Dad's family is supposed to be here midday, and Mom's panicking over the one section of the counter that has flour on it rather than being pleased that she has an entire four-course meal basically prepared and ready.

I'm in the kitchen that afternoon, waiting for the cookies I made to be done in the oven, when Dad comes in, staring down at his phone with a perplexed look in his eye.

"What's up, Dad?" I ask, reaching in to finally pull out the cookies.

"Got an email this morning from Principal Pickett," Dad says. Mom stops stirring whatever it is she's working on and looks over to him.

"And?"

"Willa Mills is missing."

We all stop what we're doing and turn to him.

"What?" I ask. "But you just saw her."

Mom's eyebrows shoot up.

"You just saw her?"

"Yeah," Dad says, rubbing his temple. "At the grocery store last night. Said she and her brother were running an errand for their mom. He waited for her in the parking lot, but she apparently never came back to the car."

My stomach drops. I don't know Willa that well, but any news like that is unnerving. And *way* too close to home. Mom walks over to Dad and puts her hand on his.

"That's awful. I'm sorry, hon. Hopefully, they'll find her soon," she says. He gives half a smile and nods. He makes his way into the living room, and we can hear his recliner creak as he plops down.

"Poor Dad," I say. Mom nods.

"I know. She's one of his best students."

News about Willa spreads like wildfire, just like any sort of news does in a small town. I've heard three different versions of the story so far: one saying she was dragged out of the parking lot while her brother tried to stop the perpetrator; another that she ran away; and another saying that she was already back home and that the whole thing wasn't true.

Unfortunately, based on the updates my Dad's getting from Principal Pickett, I know the latter isn't true. Willa is definitely missing.

Our family comes, and Dad's not himself. I watch him go through the motions, hugging, kissing, telling the little cousins how grown up they look. But his eyes are somewhere else. Willa. He's worried, and I feel for him.

Her picture is plastered all over social media, and I watch the wave of those who are *actually* friends with her post things, versus those who have seen her once and are pretending to be friends with her for the sake of having a personal involvement. I refuse to be that person. I don't really know Willa. But I want her home safe. I share the photos, adding, "Come home soon, Willa!" But I'm not going to sit here like some of my sick classmates, hoping for a "Wow, so sorry about your friend" type of response.

Everyone's cleaning up after dinner when there's a loud knock on the door. Dad excuses himself to go answer it, Mom peeking around to see who could be knocking on our door on Christmas Eve.

To our surprise, it is Brady Waylon, one of Dad's good friends from high school, and one of the members of the Tilden Police Force. He's in uniform.

"Brady?" Dad asks. "What's going on? Are you okay?" Mom appears next to Dad at the door while the rest of us peek in. The house grows eerily quiet for it being Christmas at the Porters'.

Brady clears his throat.

"Evening, Joe, Caroline," he says, nodding to my parents. "Joe, I'm sorry to have to do this on Christmas Eve, but I need to see if you can ride down to the station with me. We are working the Willa Mills case, and we have an eyewitness that places you at the same store at the time of her disappearance."

I feel my heart beating in my stomach. This doesn't feel right. Tucker squeezes into the narrow hallway next to me, and I feel him tense up, which is very out of character.

"Sure, yeah, absolutely," Dad says, leaning over to grab his hat and coat off the rack. He turns around to kiss Mom on the cheek. "I saw Willa last night. I'll help any way I can."

He turns to follow Brady out the door when Mom calls after them.

"This is just to help with the investigation, right?" Mom asks. She doesn't ask the full question, but she doesn't have to. I know what she's wondering, because I'm wondering the same thing. Is my dad in some sort of trouble for this?

"Yes, Caroline. Just protocol," Brady says. She nods and kisses Dad one more time.

"Call me if you need me to pick you up," Mom tells him. Brady nods in her direction.

"I'll bring him home," he says.

Dad turns back to Mom.

"Go on back inside, hon. Enjoy the rest of the evening. I'll be back soon," he says with a smile on his face. But as he gets into the passenger seat of Brady's squad car, I'm not quite sure that I believe him.

3

WYATT

I watched her take off from the bar like a bat out of hell, and I don't know why, but I had to follow her. Mind you, I have no idea what the fuck I'm going to say, but at least now I have the excuse of needing to go change my shirt.

I slide my hand through the elevator doors, still with no plan as to how I'm going to respond. Apologize? A bit late. And to be fair, I had a good excuse. Explain? Don't need to. She knows what happened. Ask her how she's doing? I'm pretty sure she'd slit my throat right here in this elevator.

So I just get in, finding her eyes, then posting up against the back of the elevator. I see the "27" button glowing, so I know we've got a bit of a ride. I'm on the 24th floor, but I'm not cutting this short. Not until I can get my fucking foot out of my mouth and figure out what to say. What exactly do you say to the girl whose life you tore apart all those years ago?

She steps farther away from me, crossing her arms over her chest and letting out an extra-frustrated sigh.

"What the *fuck* are you doing here?" she finally breaks the silence, her eyes staring straight ahead. The elevator ticks slowly from floor to floor.

"Well, thanks to a clumsy bar-goer, I'm in need of a clean shirt," I say, tugging on the tight cotton of my button-up. She flashes her eyes to me.

"Nothing clumsy about it. All done with intent," she says then turns back around. "I meant, what are you doing here? In Florida? At Melladon?"

"Oh, that," I say, leaning back to grasp the handrail behind me. "I'm the keynote speaker for graduation."

Her jaw drops, and she turns her head toward me.

"You've got to be fucking kidding me," she whispers. I shake my head and can't help but smile.

"No, actually. I guess they found it somewhat impressive that one of their alumni—and a minority, at that—has gained so much success before the age of thirty," I say with a smug smile. She rolls her eyes.

"Jesus Christ," she mutters, pulling her arms tighter over her chest, giving her breasts a lift—not that they need one. She's a lot more grown up than I remember. The last time I saw her was at the cemetery. She was a senior in high school, so past the awkward stage but not quite as mind-boggling as she is in this moment. Not quite the long legs, tan skin, ass-to-die-for that she has now.

But the major difference is that this version of Maryn appears to loathe me even more than the original. And I don't know why, but it's kind of hot.

"So," I say, my eyes trailing across the floor of the elevator as we approach the 20s, "how have you been?"

Her eyes flick to mine again, widening.

"How...how have I been?" she asks, her voice chillingly quiet. "How. Have. I. Been?"

I take a step back. Yikes. Might have unleashed the beast with that one. I step forward and press the 24th button, feeling like this ride might need to come to an end faster than I was hoping.

"Look, Maryn, I just..."

"You just *what*, Wyatt? Couldn't just let me have my college graduation?"

I snort.

"You really think that, after all this time, I actually remembered—or even *knew* in the first place—that you went here? And if I did know, you think I gave a damn?" I ask her. Finally, the doors open, and I step off.

But to my surprise, I hear her thick heels pounding out of the doors behind me.

"Do you know who's coming to graduation?" she asks. I keep walking down the long hall to my room. I can practically feel the heat radiating off of her body. "My fucking family. My *father*."

I stop walking and take in a deep breath. I close my eyes and turn slowly to look at her.

"I..." I start to say with a shrug. What the fuck do I say? I sigh. "I'm sorry."

I turn around again and begin walking back down this never-ending, godforsaken hallway.

"You're *sorry?*" she says, her voice getting louder with every word. "Fuck you, Wyatt. *Fuck. You.*"

I turn and look at her again over my shoulder as I finally reach my door. I've never cussed at a lady, but this one is testing me.

"Easy," I warn, holding a hand up. "Those are some fightin' words."

I watch as her eyebrows jump. She remembers the last time I said that to her just as clearly as I do. "You need to remember that we have both been through some shit."

She snorts, and I feel her getting closer and closer to me.

She pushes up against me so that we're chest to chest —or, we would be if she wasn't so short—and I can feel her breath and smell her hair, both of which have me feeling weirdly intoxicated. She has fire in her eyes, and it's lighting me up from the inside out.

"I have only been through some shit because of *you*," she says. I narrow my eyes at her, looking down at her. I don't know why I do it. I don't know what the fuck possesses me to do it, because it could go so incredibly, horribly wrong. But I wrap my hands around her head and lean down, kissing her hard. It lasts longer than I mean for it to. She reaches up and clutches onto my wrists for a moment, and I push my tongue into her mouth.

Jesus, that hate tastes good.

Just as she's stirring up my insides, making my dick jump and pull toward her, she pushes away. She shoves my hands off of her face and pounds her hands against my chest, knocking me into my door.

"What the *fuck* was that?" she asks, wiping her mouth. But I'm not dumb. I can see that she's asking herself just as much as she's asking me.

"I'm sorry," I whisper, trying to slow my breathing down. But I know it's too late now. I full-on want the shit out of this girl.

"Fuck you, Wyatt," she whispers. But to my surprise, she takes a step closer to me.

"I'm sorry," I whisper again. Another step closer to me. I have my back to my wall and my hands at my sides. If she wants this—and God, I hope she does—she's going to have to make the next move. She stopped it once. I'm not pushing myself on her.

"Fuck. You."

"I'm sorry," I whisper one last time. She pushes herself up against me and presses up onto her toes, kissing me again. She wastes no time getting her tongue into my mouth, and it takes my breath away. I wrap my arms around her waist, rubbing her back, twirling my fingers through her long blonde hair. My, my, Miss Maryn has certainly grown up.

I clutch onto the back of her head, pulling her into me closer. She takes a little jump and wraps her legs around my waist, and I know she can feel what she's doing to me. I stop for a second to reach back and unlock my door. I carry her inside and shut it, pushing her up against it and kissing her neck like a fucking madman.

Jesus Christ, I hardly know this girl. But it's like this trance. I can't stop. And I'm really fucking hoping that she can't, either.

I pick her up off the door and take a few steps toward the wall beside it. I slam her back against it, kissing her neck, her shoulders, her chin, her lips. I bite her bottom lip as she moans and drops her head back against the wall, giving me perfect access to leave my mark on her. Not too dark, I tell myself, she's got graduation.

She's writhing underneath me, letting herself move up and down against me, and it's making my insides churn.

I push off the wall, and we pause for a moment, catching our breath.

Our eyes meet, and I wait anxiously for the moment she realizes what she's doing—and who she's doing it with. That fire in her eyes is still there, but it doesn't seem to be pushing her to stop.

She slides down to her feet and reaches for the hem of my shirt, pulling it out of my slacks. She swiftly unbuttons the whole thing in a second's time, sliding it down off of my arms. I watch as her eyes trail my chest and arms. She's not the only one who did some growing up. She reaches down and unbuckles my belt, pushing my pants down to the ground. And suddenly, I'm aware that I'm very close to being naked in front of her, and she's still fully dressed. I reach up and untie her top, yanking it down with one quick motion. To my pleasant surprise, she's got no bra on, and I know every inch of me is now pressing through my boxers, pointing directly at her. I reach down and unbutton her tight-ass skinny jeans, kissing her neck as I do it.

"You're gonna have to work a little magic to get these babies off," she whispers. I pull back and look at her.

"Do you want me to?" I ask. She answers by pulling me into her, plunging her tongue into my mouth and ending it with a long, slow tug on my bottom lip with her teeth.

"Do it," she says, and I waste no fucking time. In a second, she's in front of me in nothing but a pair of yellow, lacy panties, and it's taking every muscle in my body not to rip them off of her. She steps closer to me, pushing me so that I'm up against the bed. She puts a hand on my chest and shoves me down onto it. I'm on my back now, bracing for her.

She climbs up my body slowly—painfully slow—her eyes fixated on mine. She gets to me and leans down to kiss me again.

"I've hated you for so fucking long," she whispers, nibbling at my earlobe. The sensation gives me chills and makes me tighten my grip on her ass.

"I know," I whisper back. She bends her head to kiss my neck, sucking on it gently. *Careful,* I think, *graduation is coming.*

"I still do," she whispers. I nod, my eyes closed, rolling back in my head as she licks and bites.

"I know," I whisper again. Suddenly, her hands are at the rim of my boxers, and she pulls them down, letting me spring free.

"I wanted you to be miserable," she says, kissing my jawline and letting her fingers trail down my stomach. I groan when she grabs all of me, pumping her hand up and down as she does. I let her work for a moment, then I flip her over so that I'm on top.

"I know," I whisper again. I slide my fingers down into the top of her panties, down until I find the deepest, wettest part of her. And I've just gotten confirmation that she wants me as badly as I want her.

I slide my fingers down between her folds, letting them explore for a moment before plunging them inside of her. She gasps, clawing at my back and biting my chest.

I go wild for a moment inside of her until she stops me and rolls me back over.

"You ruined everything," she says, staring into my eyes. I swallow. This isn't exactly my idea of dirty talk, but it would be pretty hard to kick the Maryn-high I'm on right now. I reach up and grab her face, pulling it toward mine.

"I know," I whisper again, leaving a trail of kisses from behind her ear, up her jawline. "But for the record, I've always hoped you were happy."

She pushes back, staring at me for a moment.

Then, to my very-pleasant surprise, she slides down onto me, so perfectly quick that I feel dizzy.

And then, she rides the shit out of me, kissing me hard, biting my lip, sucking on my neck. I feel her nails digging into my back, her legs pressing into me, her whole body clenching around me. I can feel how conflicted she is, like she wants to hurt me but she needs me at the same time. I feel myself getting close, but I'm not ready for this to end. I don't know what the fuck this crazy, hate sex is, but I know I'd be a fool to think this is going to happen more than once. As she has reminded me several times, she hates me to my core.

She just has a weird way of showing it.

I let her rock back and forth a moment longer before flipping her onto her back. I get up on my knees and pull her legs up onto my shoulders. Her tan skin looks a little brighter against my dark chest, and every inch of her looks fucking delicious. I pound back into her, and she loses it, panting and clawing at the sheets. And in the most beautiful sound of my fucking life, she calls out my name—heavy, breathy, subconsciously. Her eyes close as she breathes in and out. I let myself release and then fall to the bed next to her.

I pull her into my chest, spooning her, our bodies breathing in sync. She draws in a long, slow breath then pulls my arms around her tighter.

4
———

MARYN

I wake up, eyes fluttering. This is not my finest moment, because I actually don't remember where I am. As I become more aware of my surroundings, I feel the weight of an arm across my body, and I look down.

I see the mocha-brown of his skin, the bulging veins.

Oh, that's right. I fucked Wyatt Mills.

The man who ruined everything. *Everything.*

I gasp audibly as I remember the last evening's occurrences, including the most intense orgasm of my life, and move like crazy to get out of the bed. I run across the room, picking up my clothes and throwing them on.

"What's going on?" he asks groggily, pushing himself up and rubbing his eyes. God damn, he's hot. He was one of the only mixed kids in town; his dad was the first black football player to get a scholarship from Tilden High School. His green eyes came from his mom. And his sister...well, she was just as beautiful as he is.

But I have no time to admire. I need to get out of

here, back to my apartment, to get ready for the influx of family and graduation festivities.

And I need to get back to hating Wyatt Mills and pretending like last night never fucking happened.

I turn to him as I secure my messy bun with a hair tie.

"I can't believe we..." I start to say. I stop and grab my bag off of the floor. I make a beeline for the door, but he calls my name.

"Maryn," he says, his morning voice still smooth as ever. I take in a deep breath and turn to him slowly.

"Last night was a huge fucking mistake," I say without lifting my eyes to him. Then, I charge out of his door and toward the elevator. I have approximately one million texts from my friends. The last is from Ellie.

If you don't answer in the next hour, we're calling the cops, it says. I dial her.

"Where the fuck are you?" she answers. Keely is in the background.

"Yeah. You better have a good explanation, bitch," she says.

"I have an explanation, but I'm not sure it's good," I tell them as I tap my foot anxiously, waiting for the elevator to get here. "Please tell me you guys haven't left the hotel yet."

"We're in the lobby," Ellie says. "Hurry up."

I get off the elevator and see the two of them looking almost as bad as I do. Except, they stayed to drink longer, so they might actually look worse.

Me, I'm just hungover on the viciously amazing sex I had with the man of my nightmares.

"What the fuck? Where were you?" Keely asks, thrusting a cup of coffee at me.

I take a sip and look up at them.

"In someone's room," I say sheepishly.

"Someone? Like, a guy?" Ellie asks. I nod, putting a hand to my head.

"What, are we playing twenty questions?" Keely asks. "Who the fuck was it?"

I draw in a long, slow breath then look up at them.

"Wyatt Mills," I mutter. I give them a moment, waiting for them to catch on. They aren't from my hometown. The Mills-Porter fiasco wasn't such a big deal down here.

"Wait, is that the dude who—" Keely starts. Ellie gasps.

"No fucking *way*," she says. "The guy who...your parents...oh my *God!*"

"Shh, I know, I know," I whisper. "I'll tell you all about it, but can we please talk in the car? I have no idea when he's coming down here, and I don't want to be here when he does."

They nod, and we check out and get back in Keely's car.

"Okay, so how the *fuck* did this happen?" she asks, looking at me through the rearview mirror as she begins to pull out of the lot.

"I honestly have no idea," I say, staring out the window.

It's true. One minute, I was seething. I was picturing his death in more ways than one. I was remembering the fear, the pain our family felt for months because of him.

And then, the next, all I wanted was his body. Like I wanted to take something from him. Keep a part of him for myself or something. It was animalistic. Weird.

"Is he, like, really hot?" Keely asks. Ellie gasps again.

"Holy shit—yeah he is!" she says, letting Keely look at his Facebook picture on her phone. I moan and cover my eyes with my arm.

"But I thought you, like, hated his guts? I mean, isn't he the reason you almost didn't get to come to college in the first place?" Keely asks. I moan again.

"Yeah, he is," I mutter behind my arm.

"You know what this means," Ellie says, turning to me with a smug look on her face.

"What?" I ask.

"It means you just had *the* dick," she says matter-of-factly. I see Keely's eyebrows shoot up in the mirror. I shake my head.

"No, it does not," I say. But they both start laughing and smiling, making tormenting sounds at my expense.

"Oh, yes, it does," Ellie says. "So, the next time you want to ask me why I keep letting Dickson into my pants, remember last night. Remember how badly you wanted him—so badly that you forgot everything he ever did to you."

I swallow.

"Okay, Miss Thing," Keely says. "I know you're not about to let what she just did validate the fact that you're still fucking someone's husband." Ellie swallows, and I cross my arms over my chest and smirk at her through the mirror. "And *you*," Keely says, eyeing me now, "next time you want to go on one of your judgmental tangents, remember last night."

I moan again, sinking down into the seat.

A few hours pass, and I'm staring at my naked self in the mirror. My parents and brother are going to be here within the hour, and we have reservations at one of the nicest restaurants in town. But all I can seem to do is stare at the hickey Wyatt left on my chest. Normally, I'd be panicking, trying foundation and a cold spoon—all the old tricks—but he left this one low enough that no one will see it. And even if they could, there's something about it that entrances me, reminds me of last night. For the briefest of moments, he was mine, and I was his. And I will never, *ever* say this out loud, but it felt good. For a moment.

There's a knock on the door.

"You almost done in there?" Keely asks. "Some of us have to pee."

"Yeah, sorry," I say, reaching down to grab my dress and put it on.

"So," Keely says, sitting down on the toilet before I'm even out the door, "I assume you won't be telling the fam about your run-in?"

I scoff from the hallway.

"Fuck no, and you better not, either," I say. She laughs.

"Well, no shit. Hopefully, you won't run into him again before graduation."

I nod. Then my eyes get wide. Shit. Graduation.

Keynote speaker.

Oh, fuck me.

"Fuck," I say, plopping down on the couch and dropping my face into my hands.

"What?" she says, following me out after she washes her hands.

"He's the fucking keynote speaker," I mumble.

"What?" she asks.

"He's the fucking keynote speaker," I say again, loud and clear. She steps back.

"What? How? Why? Why would that be?" Keely

asks. She stalks over to the kitchen table and sits down, opening her laptop. She types away for a moment.

"'Commencement speaker will be Mr. Wyatt Mills, graduate of Melladon, 2015. Mr. Mills was recently named Vice President at a public relations agency in Manhattan and has still made time to run a foundation for families of missing and murdered persons,'" Keely reads from the school-wide email that I got and promptly ignored. She looks up at me.

Ugh. Murdered persons.

Wait. Public relations agency?

"What agency?" I ask.

"Please hold," Keely says as she searches his name. Her eyes get wide, and she bites down on her thumbnail. "'Wyatt Mills named Vice President at Caldell Communications,'" she reads the headline.

Caldell Communications. As in, the place where I'm supposed to launch my career in just a few short weeks if this next interview goes well.

Fucking great.

"No fucking way," I say. "No goddamn, fucking, shit-ass way!"

"Calm your tits," Keely says, closing the computer and coming back over to me and sitting down on the couch. I'm starting to feel lightheaded. I can feel this weight pushing down on my chest.

In just a few hours, he will be standing in front of thousands of us, my parents included, while he talks about the hardships he's faced and how he's overcome them.

He will be there, back in New York, in just a few weeks, while I attempt to become a grown-up.

Oh, and he screwed me silly last night.

All of which I have about ten minutes to get over before Mom and Dad get here.

"Bitch," Keely says, taking my face in her hands. "Calm. The. Eff. Down. Seriously. You're giving this guy way too much power." I suck in a long breath and open my eyes.

"What?"

"It's only been a few hours since you saw him last. But before that, it had been *years*. And look at you—a sweaty, anxiety-ridden mess. Seriously, fuck this guy. I mean, not literally, you already tried that and look at you now."

I narrow my eyes at her and shove her shoulder as she cackles.

"I mean it, though, Mare. Give your parents a warning that he will be speaking. You guys will get through it. Celebrate your graduation, because you've worked your ass off. Don't let him have this."

I nod.

"Yeah, okay," I say just as there are about thirty-seven overly enthusiastic knocks on our apartment door.

"Good girl. Now, showtime for Mommy and Daddy," Keely says, standing up to greet my family.

MY PARENTS HAVE BEEN an emotional wreck since they got to Florida. My brother is soaking in all the sights and sounds of the Florida college life; he just finished his freshman year at a small school in Pennsylvania, and he's having a blast. But my parents…they can't believe I'm done. They keep saying how proud they are, keep telling me they wish I didn't have to take out all those loans, keep telling me how amazing it is that I already have a job prospect.

"Oh, baby, I just wish we could have——" Mom starts again at dinner. I take a sip of my wine and roll my eyes.

"Ma, please," I say. "It's fine. A lot of kids take out loans. That's just par for the course for my generation, okay?"

"I know, honey. It's not just the loans. I just wish you didn't have to go through college with such a cloud over your head."

My dad looks down at his plate and clears his throat. I swallow.

I know what cloud she means. She means Wyatt Mills.

The cloud that was between my thighs last night. I swallow and take another nervous sip of wine. Then I shrug.

"There was no cloud. There *is* no cloud," I say. "Everything is back to normal. I refuse to let any 'clouds' control my life."

Mom smiles and nods, and Dad squeezes my hand from across the table.

"Proud of you, kid," he says. I swallow again. I guess this is the best time to mention it—not that any time is good.

"But on that note," I say, my voice shaky. "We got an email from school about some graduation details. And, well, there was some information about the commence-ment speaker."

Dad raises an eyebrow.

"Oh? Someone good, I hope?"

"Oh! Is it Oprah? Or maybe Ellen?" Mom asks. I laugh nervously and shake my head.

"Actually," I say, "it's a Melladon alumnus. Remember that 'cloud' we were talking about?"

Dad puts his drink down on the table, and the glass hits so hard I'm sure it's going to break. Mom's eyes are wide, and even Tucker has brought his attention back to the table instead of our waitress's ass.

"Yes…" Dad says.

"Yeah, well, the particular alumnus speaking is none other than Wyatt Mills himself," I say, leaving out the part about him practically running the place where I might be working.

Mom blinks a thousand times in a minute, while Dad just stares at me blankly. It's like they didn't hear me.

"Whoa," Tucker says, "what are the fucking chances?"

Mom's head whips to Tucker.

"Language," she says. He rolls his eyes.

"Are you...are you kidding me?" Dad says, and I feel my heartrate accelerate. I shake my head.

"Unfortunately not. He graduated before I even got to Melladon. Apparently, he runs some support group for families of missing and, uh, murdered people."

I let the information sink in for a minute.

"I'm really sorry, guys," I say. Mom laughs nervously and puts her hand on mine.

"Oh, honey," she says, "it's not your fault. What a horrible coincidence. It's like the universe is playing some trick on us."

"Damn, that'll be fun to watch," Dad says sarcastically. Then, he throws an arm around my shoulders. "But yeah, hon, it's not like it's your fault."

I smile and nod.

"Yeah," I manage to mutter.

"Well, I guess it could be worse," Dad says. "I guess we should be thankful you're not bringing him home to us or something!"

With that, he and Mom share an uncomfortable laugh. I join in, guzzling down my wine like it's my only lifeline, because right now, I'm pretty sure it is.

5

DECEMBER 2014 - WYATT

I can't breathe. That's all I keep thinking.

We've been at the police station for hours now, and they just keep asking us the same questions. I've walked them through the evening's events what feels like twenty times. The detective keeps asking if I'm forgetting anything.

But I can barely see straight, let alone think straight. I'm a senior in college. This is my last semester break before graduation. My last Christmas living at home with my parents. And my sister.

I keep running through the trip to the store like something new is going to stand out to me.

One second, she was here with me. Texting me back. Telling me she was waiting in line.

The next, she wasn't answering my texts or calls.

I saw her walk out of the store. I looked down at my phone to finish texting Brenna. I looked up. Willa was gone. There was some sort of dark SUV speeding away.

But Willa was gone.

When I went into the store, no one had seen her.

There were only a few people left shopping and not a single person saw her.

When I ran around the parking lot, she was nowhere. When I got in my car and drove circles around the perimeter of the shopping center, she was nowhere. When I called her twenty-three more times, she was still nowhere.

I called 911, then my parents, all in shock.

And now we're here.

"Son, is there *anything* you remember? Did you happen to get a glimpse of the make or model of the SUV, maybe? The license plate? Anyone seem out of sorts?" the tall, big-boned lady detective asks me again. My dad squeezes my shoulders as my mom takes my hand. "Did you see anyone you recognized? Or anyone you didn't, that might have seemed like they didn't belong?"

I lean forward, holding my head between my hands and rubbing my temples.

I pulled up to the side of the store and let Willa out while I drove around to find parking.

I watched her walk around toward the front of the store.

She was waving to someone, then she disappeared.

Wait.

That teacher.

She was waving to that teacher. The history guy. I didn't have him in high school, but a lot of my friends did.

"She saw a teacher she knew. Mr. Porter, I think his name was," I say.

"Joe Porter?" another male cop asks.

"I guess so, teaches history at the high school."

The cop nods.

"Do we know what kind of car Joe Porter drives?" the lady detective asks the cop. The cop swallows.

"I believe he has a navy-blue Explorer," the cop says. Mom's eyes grow wide.

The two cops excuse themselves, and I feel this twinge of uncertainty in my belly. Mr. Porter seemed like a decent guy. But my sister's missing, and he saw her last. I look at my mom. This is the first time all night she hasn't been actively crying. Something's replacing the tears in her eyes, and I'm pretty sure it's hope.

Yeah. Let's focus on this Porter guy.

6

WYATT

I've been walking around like a zombie since this morning when Maryn Porter bolted out of my room after what was the best sex I've ever had.

I can't get out of this slump. Now, I'm slowly dressing myself for this graduation ceremony, but it feels like it's in the way far off future rather than in just a few hours. I've agonized over this speech for weeks, read through it a million times. And yet, somehow, this morning, I don't seem to give a damn about it.

I had no idea she went here. Honestly. Our families weren't exactly in close touch after everything, and there were two distinctive groups in town: one that supported her father and her family, and one that supported mine. They did a good job of keeping the divide strong, and in turn, keeping our families pretty separate.

I felt a moment of guilt when she mentioned that her family would be here, watching, listening to me.

But then I quickly let it go when I remembered my mom and dad would be here, too. Listening to me give my speech, smiling up at me. Their only child.

Well, the only one that's left.

But I still can't shake her. I can't shake her blue eyes burning holes through me. I can't shake these scratch marks down my back. I can't get over the number of times she told me she hated me, and how each time, all it made me want to do was kiss her.

I look at myself in the mirror as I tie my tie. I want to bitch-slap myself. *Get over it, dude,* I tell myself. *You're a successful partner at one of the best communication firms in the city. You make six figures before thirty, have a great group of friends —which includes a few super-hot ladies who are more than happy to escort you back to your apartment on a regular basis. You've got it all.*

But despite my little motivational talk, I know it's all for nothing. Because Maryn Porter is on my mind, and the remnants of my one night with her are still all over me, no many how many showers I take.

She hates me, and I get it.

But I can't hate her back. I never could. And now I know I never will.

I sigh as I straighten out my suit in the mirror. I rub my head. As my phone buzzes with a text from my mom, I head out of my hotel room door.

Soon, I'll be back in New York, back to work, back to my life pre-Maryn. And yet, I know nothing will feel like it was.

"WELL, DON'T YOU LOOK HANDSOME," Mom says as she tugs gently on my tie. Her blonde hair has a hint of gray in it now, and the lines near her eyes are more prominent. But she's still such a beautiful woman.

Willa was so much like her.

Man, I miss Willa.

"Thanks, Mama," I say, leaning down to kiss her cheek.

"You clean up like your daddy," Pops says, clapping my back. I smile.

"Well, let's get to this," I say, leading them out the doors to wave down a cab.

"I am just so proud of you," Mom says, fluffing her hair in the back of the cab. "I mean it. For you to be chosen out of all their alumni—wow. You have just changed so many people's lives."

I put my hand on her knee.

"Thanks, Mom," I say.

"People will be blown away," Dad says from the passenger seat, his hand out the window.

"I don't know if everyone will," I say quietly. I feel like this is as good of a time as any. They're going to see her walk across the stage soon. They deserve fair warning.

"What do you mean, boy?" Dad asks, his dark skin making his tan suit look extra classy. I sigh.

"I didn't realize it till last night, but apparently, I'm not the only one from Tilden who went here," I say. "Apparently, Maryn Porter is graduating today."

Mom's eyes get wide, and Dad turns around in his seat so quickly that it makes our driver jump.

"What?" Mom says in a whisper. I nod.

"Yeah, weird coincidence," I say. I chuckle. "What are the chances?"

Dad whistles and shakes his head.

"Damn," he says, "what are the friggin' chances?"

"So her, um, family…" Mom starts to say. I can see the nerves building inside of her, filling her eyes. I nod.

"Yeah, I'm sure they will be here," I say. She nods. "But there are three thousand kids graduating today. It should be easy to avoid them."

"Well," Dad says, clearing his throat and running his hand across his goatee, "I wish them all the best."

Me too, Pops. Me too.

I LEAVE my parents at the front of the building and head back to where I'm supposed to meet the class sponsors and administration. They give me the rundown of where I'll be sitting onstage, who will introduce me, and where to go.

"And then you'll stand in line to shake the graduates' hands," the sponsor tells me, pointing to the chair onstage where I will be sitting. I whip my head back to her.

"I'll be shaking their hands? All of them?" I ask. She smiles and nods.

"Of course. You're the guest of honor. You'll be a part of the receiving line."

I swallow.

I'm going to touch Maryn Porter again today. And in front of her parents.

The ceremony goes by painfully slow. I scan the crowd to try to find her, but I can't make her out amongst all the faces. Finally, it's my turn for the speech, and I'm uncharacteristically nervous. This isn't like me. I'm always so smooth. But I know she's watching. And so is her dad.

I take a deep breath and let it go.

I talk about my time here at school and about how college helped me recover from the loss of my sister.

I talk about how I graduated top of my class. But then I talk about how none of that mattered without Willa.

I talk about how I decided to do something about it, because I knew there were others like me, suffering without their family members, their friends. Missing them every single day, feeling unworthy to live their lives. I can hear the sniffles from the audience, and I know it's hitting them. I wonder if it's hitting Maryn.

Finally, I get to the last line—the clincher.

"What I've learned from the loss of my sister is to pull those closest to you even closer," I say. "Lean on them. Depend on them, and be someone they can depend on. Let yourself have those days of uncertainty, those moments of self-doubt. But then, get yourself together. Pull yourself back up. Remember how worthy you are of every single day you're given on this earth. Take time to learn your purpose, and then go after it. Don't let anything make you too afraid to live. Thank you."

Everyone rises to their feet, clapping and cheering, smiling, whistling. I wave, shake the dean's hand, and take my seat next to one of the department chairs.

I wait another excruciating hour before the names are called, and we finally reach the P's. I see her lining up on the side of the stage. And as she makes her way to the top of the stairs on the right side, her eyes catch mine. I'm anxious, on fire, ready to feel that zap again when our skin touches. But the look on her face tells me she's anything but excited. She looks nervous—terrified, even.

Nothing like the bold sex goddess she was mere

hours ago. And Jesus, she even makes a graduation cap look good.

"Maryn Alyse Porter, *Summa Cum Laude,*" the dean reads. Alyse. I love that. I know the audience is clapping, but I don't hear them. I just hear the blood rushing through my body as I extend my hand to her. She looks down at it for a moment, then lets her eyes scan the crowd. She takes it for only a second, our eyes meeting for the briefest of moments, then she nods and continues her way down the line.

"Ms. Porter," I call out, causing a bit of a backup in the line. She looks at me, eyes wide. "Congratulations."

She nods again before waving out to her family in the crowd then making her way down the other side of the stage.

And I know that's it for us.

A FEW DAYS PASS, and I'm slowly getting over my night with Maryn. I've finally stopped picturing her naked at random times. Finally stopped getting that tingle in my dick when I remember her telling me how much she hated me and then kissing me better than I'd ever been kissed.

I'm back in New York, back in the swing of things. Still getting used to my corner office, my new digs. I have a personal assistant, which, to be honest, I'm still not comfortable with yet. And I have a fucking phenomenal view of Central Park.

Life is good. There's nothing missing, no unfinished business at all.

I'm staring out the window, chucking a Yankees ball

up and down at my desk when there's a knock on my door.

"Hey, man," Nate says as he pops his head in. Nate's the CFO of the company, for no other reason, I'm convinced, than the fact that his dad is the CEO. Although, to be fair, his dad made him work his ass off for this position. And he's actually good with money. So it works.

"Hey, Nate," I say, popping up to shake his hand. He takes a seat in the chair across from my desk.

"How was the trip back to the old stomping grounds?" he asks. "Any hot college chicks after ya?"

I smile and shake my head, one last flash of her naked body under mine going through my brain.

"Oh, tons," I say with a chuckle. "How were things here?"

"Not bad," he says. "We closed the deal with Landry, thanks to you." I nod and press my lips out. Landry Hotels has been a top prospect for us for a few years. And after a few lunches with their CEO and director of marketing, I was finally able to land the account. The deal was signed and sealed last week while I was away.

"Fucking awesome," I say, clapping my hands together.

"Yeah, man. Thanks to you," he says, standing up. "It's gonna be a good year. Oh, and we narrowed down the candidates for that coordinator position." He drops two folders on my desk.

"These are the resumes. I know that position will work with your team a lot, so we wanted to make sure you got a chance to review them. Let me know which you think is most qualified."

I nod and thank him, picking up the two folders as he heads out the door.

The first candidate is Tommy Jensen, a recent graduate from Boston University. His interning experience is actually impressive, but his writing test isn't super moving. I close his folder and open the second, and my jaw drops to my desk.

Fucking Maryn Porter.

Graduate of Melladon University. Alumnus of Tilden High School.

The best goddamn lay I've ever had.

I swallow, blinking to make sure my vision is clear. But it is. It's definitely her.

She interned at three different communications companies down in Florida and volunteered at a local animal shelter during her free time. Her references all gave her excellent marks, and she was the president of two different honor societies.

She's definitely qualified—in more ways than one.

I practically lunge for my desk phone and dial Nate's extension.

"Hey, man," I say. "Listen, let's go ahead and make the offer to this Porter girl."

"Make the offer? We were going to set up another interview—"

"Nah, I like her resume. Her intern experience will be really good for this position. Plus, her writing test was a lot stronger than the other guy. Let's go ahead and give it to her. And while we're at it, see if you can fund the position for a few thousand extra. Hopefully we can keep this position filled a little longer than the typical entry-level position so we won't have to retrain someone so fast."

I try and keep my voice calm and not let the urgency that's settled inside of me rise to the surface.

"Good deal, man," he says. "I'll have HR give her a call today."

I thank him and hang up.

Maybe that moment on the stage won't be the end of me and Miss Porter.

7

MARYN

I have no idea how I accumulated so much shit over the last four years, but getting this stuff back to New York has been a nightmare. I'm hoping I won't be staying at my parents' for long, but until I have a set job, my childhood bedroom is all the space I have. There are boxes stacked everywhere (most of which I know won't budge until I move out), clothes thrown in piles at every corner, and another few boxes stacked in the garage.

I take a break from unpacking—or, at least, from trying to find some clean underwear—and make my way downstairs. My phone rings, and I see Keely's face pop up on the screen. I walk outside to the backyard and answer.

"Hey, bitch," she says, shoveling a spoonful of something into her mouth. "I fucking miss you already."

"Me, too!" I hear Trey call from somewhere in the background. I smile as I sit down on our deck steps.

"I miss you guys, too," I say. I sigh. I've been avoiding thinking about it, but leaving Keely and Ellie is going to be really, really hard. I don't have many friends left here in Tilden. This small Long Island town is just that—*small*. So small it's suffocating. Once people take a stance on something, it's pretty tough to change their mind. My family learned that the hard way.

I listen to Keely talk about her new teaching job and Trey's interview that he has next week. They both want to stay down in Florida; she's only about an hour from her parents, and Trey is having much better luck with his applications there than in Georgia where he's from.

"Have you talked to Ellie?" Keely asks.

"Not since I've been home. Why?"

"Looks like she got a love note from Mrs. Dickson," Keely says, her eyebrows shooting up, prompting me to ask for more.

"What?"

"Yup. She saw the texts on his phone. He, apparently, put her name in as 'Phone Company.' Like, what an idiot, right? So she wanted to know why the phone company was sending him pictures of tits. She, apparently, apprehended the good professor's phone and contacted Ellie herself. It's over. She's not doing great," Keely says. I shake my head.

"Oh, Ellie," I say, rubbing my temples.

"Yeah. She keeps mentioning she wants to come up there and see you. Maybe you should give her a call," Keely says. I nod. It would actually be nice to have Ellie here. It's funny being back in Tilden. I've lived here my whole life, with the exception of college, yet I feel like a total transplant. God, I can't wait to move out to the city.

"I will. How are you guys doing?" I ask. Keely smiles.

"Good! We're finally going out tonight," she says. "We haven't been able to have a night out since before exams started."

I see Trey in the background, raising his eyebrows at me. Oh, my God. Tonight's the night. *The* night. My best friend is getting engaged.

I smile and nod, trying to look as casual as possible.

"Awesome, good for you guys," I say. "You guys deserve a night out."

"What about you? Any dating prospects back in New York, or are you still hung up on Mills?" Keely asks matter-of-factly.

"Shh!" I scold, looking back to make sure that I still see my parents inside the living room window. "Jesus, Keel."

"Oops," she says, covering her mouth. "Sorry, I forgot you're back with Mom and Pops." I roll my eyes.

"No, I am most definitely not still hung up on him," I say just above a whisper. "But I've only been back in New York for a few days. Let me get settled first before you start asking about my dating life."

"Fair enough." Keely shrugs. Just then, my phone starts buzzing, and I see another incoming call. It's a city area code.

"Hey, Keel, gotta run. This could be one of the jobs I applied for," I say.

"Okay, love you, bitch," she says.

"Love you. Have fun tonight!" I say, clicking over. "Hello, this is Maryn," I say, immediately switching over to my professional voice.

"Hi, Maryn, this is Beth Wilms with Caldell Communications," she says. I swallow. Caldell. Wyatt.

"Oh, hi, yes, hello," I say.

"Is this a good time?" she asks.

"Perfect."

"Great. Well, a few of our executives have reviewed your resume, and you passed the initial screening with flying colors. We'd like to offer the account coordinator position to you."

I swallow. A few of the executives? Which ones?

"Oh, wow, my goodness," I say. "So there won't be a second interview?"

"Nope, our executive team was really pleased with the results of your writing test and impressed by your internship experience. They all feel like you'd be a great fit here. Oh, and the position has been funded for extra compensation, so the salary is a bit higher than what we previously discussed. I'll send that over with your official offer letter."

I swallow again. I'm frozen. I want this job. I need it. I need to get out of Tilden, into my own life.

But that means Wyatt comes along with it.

"So," Beth finally says after a long pause, "would you like to call us back with your final answer?"

"Oh, um, yes, please, thank you so much," I say.

"Okay, great. You still have my number, so just give me a call back when you're ready."

"Will do," I say. I fumble to hang it up then dial Keely back immediately.

"Hello?" she answers.

"It was them. The company he works for. They offered me the job without a second interview, and they...*he* got me more money." There's a pause.

"God damn, you must have screwed the *shit* out of him!" Keely says.

"Keely! This is serious. I don't know what to do."

"Wait…you don't know what to *do?* You mean you haven't accepted it yet?"

"No. How can I? It feels like I'm sleeping my way into this. This is wrong, isn't it?"

"Look, bitch. You got the first interview without having a connection with him, didn't you?"

"Yes," I say.

"And you passed the first screening and the writing test without him, right?"

"Right," I say, "but—"

"And did you or did you not graduate with the highest honors? Top of your class, president of all the etas and zetas?"

I pause for a moment and sigh.

"Yes."

"Okay, then. Hook-up or not, you deserve this job with or without his input. This is your chance. You don't want to be in that shitty little town any longer than you need to be. You've worked your ass off for four years. Take it. Maybe have some storage-closet nookie or something."

"Keely!"

She laughs on the other end.

"Okay, okay, maybe no nookie. But maybe take the opposite route."

"What do you mean?"

"Don't you dare let him storm back into your life and take even more away from you. Take the job, and show him up with your skills. Shit, make *him* worry for *his* job."

I sit back on the deck step, thinking about all she's saying. I picture myself slapping an empty box on his desk, telling him to pack up his shit. It's my desk now.

But then I picture him grabbing me by the collar of my shirt and splaying me out over said desk. Ripping my clothes off. . .

No. Fuck you, Mr. Mills—and not literally.

At least, not again.

"Yeah, maybe you're right," I say. "I'm gonna call them back. Thanks, Keel."

"You got it," she says.

I tap my foot anxiously as I wait for Beth to pick up the phone.

"Caldell Communications, how can I help you?"

"Hi, Beth?"

"Yes?"

"This is Maryn Porter," I say.

"Oh, hi, Maryn, good to hear from you so quickly."

"Yes. I just wanted to gratefully accept the position," I say.

"Oh, wonderful! We are so excited to have you on the team. I'll send over your official offer, and then you'll be getting a hard copy in the mail as well. Can you start two weeks from tomorrow?"

"Yes, absolutely," I say.

"Great! We're looking forward to it!"

"Thanks again," I say. I hit end and go inside.

"Mom, Pop," I say, "I have some news."

They come around the corner from the living room into the kitchen where I'm standing.

"What's up, kid?"

"I just got a job," I say. Mom shrieks and Dad claps his hands excitedly. Tucker comes down the steps to see what the commotion is then high-fives me.

"Oh, this is so exciting! Tell us all about it!" Mom says. I give them the rundown of the company and what

I'll be doing. I tell them when I'll be starting. And totally leave out the part that Wyatt Mills will be one of the executives at the new company. What they don't know won't hurt them. I think.

"Wow, hon, this is such good news," Dad says, squeezing my shoulder.

"So, are you still thinking you'll want to move out to the city?" Mom asks. I nod.

"Yeah, I'm going to try to start looking tomorrow. I'm hoping I can find somewhere soon so I can get settled."

Mom nods, a sad look in her eyes even though she's smiling.

"I wish you didn't have to go so soon," she says, her voice soft. "But I know Tilden hasn't been your favorite place."

I nod. I wish I didn't hate being here so much, either.

It's not my family. Lord knows, these three are my everything. I'd do anything for them—as proven by some of my not-so-adult actions during the case. But I can't stay here. I can't be forced to face that time over and over again, every time I get home. I need to get to the big, loud city where I can't hear the small-town chatter.

"Yeah, Mom. Thanks," I say.

"So, what about a roommate?" Dad asks, swiftly changing the subject as he so often does. "You're not planning on living alone, right?"

"Well, I hadn't gotten that far yet, but…"

"Well, get that far, girl," Mom says. "You'll be able to afford something in a better neighborhood if you can split the rent with someone. And I won't have to worry about you all the time if I know you're not alone."

I roll my eyes and smile.

"I can put out an ad," I say. "Or ask around online."

"Gee, that sounds safe," Dad says. I chuckle.

"I'll figure it out."

"Good. Don't make us worry," Mom says, kissing my head. "We're so proud of you, babe."

"Thanks, guys."

Later that night, I manage to climb over all the shit on my floor and make it to my bed. I'm lying with my feet up against the wall, scrolling through Facebook, when I see a dramatic quote posted by Ellie.

I roll over to my stomach and dial her.

"Hello?" she answers, her voice solemn.

"I heard the good professor screwed you over," I say. She sighs.

"Yeah. I guess I screwed myself over. You guys were right. Congratulations," she says.

"Ell, we didn't want to be right. We just didn't want you to hurt anyone, or get hurt yourself," I say.

"Well, I did both. I fucked up," she says. There's a long pause, because, yeah, she did fuck up. Yeah, she had warning, words of reason in her ear that she ignored.

"Well, what are your plans now?" I ask her.

"I don't know. I want to get out of Florida. My apartment lease is up in three weeks, and I just...I don't know. I was actually thinking…"

"Come up to New York and move in with me," I say so she doesn't have to. She pauses.

"Wait...really?"

"Yes. I got that job, and I need to get out of Tilden.

I need to get my butt to Manhattan, and I don't want to go alone."

I can almost hear her smile through the phone.

"I don't have a job yet, but I'm sure my parents would cover my rent for a few months until I found something," she says. I smile. Her parents have been "covering" her expenses for as long as I've known her. And I don't mean, like, tuition and food. I mean, like, her couple-grand-a-month clothing bill, a new car every year…that kind of thing. But if they are going to pay half my rent, I'm cool with that.

"Good. Call them and get your butt up here. We have an apartment to hunt," I say. I hear her sniff on the other end of the line. Keely is my tough, strong, head-on-straight, shit-together friend. Ellie is my soft, sensitive, will-hold-you-in-the-middle-of-the-night friend. She's a little lost because no one has ever pushed her to find herself. But she's got a good soul.

"Thank you, Mare," she says. "I need this."

ELLIE CALLED HER PARENTS AND, within a week, had her bags packed, a flight to New York booked, and was on her way. I picked her up at JFK, and we've been crashing at my parents' in between visits to the city to apartment hunt. So far, everything we've seen has been no bigger than a cardboard box, too far from the office for me, or—my mom's favorite—"not the best neighbor-hood." I scroll down in one of my rental apps, and my eyes grow wide.

"What about this one?" I ask, handing Ellie my phone as I take over stirring the brownie batter.

"Whoa," she says. "How far is this from work?"

"Not," I say. "Walkable, but I can take the train if it's nasty out."

"Call!" she says, thrusting the phone back to me. I dial the number quickly, and we book a tour for tomorrow morning.

That night, as we lie in my double-bed, Ellie rolls over to me.

"Are you ready to see him again?" she asks. I swallow and squeeze my eyes shut.

"No," I say. "I'm not." She thinks about it for a moment.

"Well, I'm really proud of you for taking this job," she says. I look at her. "I'm proud of you for not letting him screw with your life more than he already has. I know this is going to be great for you, Mare." I squeeze her hand.

"I hope you're right," I say, rolling onto my side and trying desperately to bury the fear of seeing Wyatt every day for the foreseeable future.

8

JANUARY 2015 - MARYN

E very morning for the last few weeks, I wake up and I feel like I'm in some sort of weird, alternate universe where everything has been flipped on its head. Mom is swamped, doing all the shopping, cooking, and cleaning, basically on her own. Tucker and I try to help outside of school and homework, but I'm afraid we don't have a whole lot of time to offer.

Dad is basically a ghost of himself. Ever since the cops showed up on our doorstep, nothing in this house has been the same.

They took him to the station that night, and from what Tucker and I overheard him telling Mom from the steps, they essentially interrogated him.

An "eyewitness" placed him at the scene of the crime, speaking to the victim, and that's all the Tilden police seemed to need. Dad hired a lawyer pretty quickly after, which I heard him tell Mom is going to cost them an arm and a leg. His lawyer instructed him not to reach out to the Mills family, which I think is torturing him on a whole other level. My dad has been an educator for almost 25 years. He cares about his students like any good teacher does. He's not the "leave when the bell rings" kind of teacher. He's the "leave when the kids have learned and the job is done" sort of teacher. And now, one of his best students is missing. And he can't grieve like he wants to, offer support like he needs to, because he's on the borderline of being accused of having something to do with it.

So far, things have been pretty quiet about Dad's involvement, but Mom says we're just waiting for the bubble to burst. I hope she's wrong. But this is Tilden, population 3,000. Three thousand people that have nothing better to do than to wait for someone else's scandal to crack so that they can pounce and ignore their own problems.

Dad's still driving me to school every day, but our rides are a lot quieter. We haven't stopped for donuts in a while, and he doesn't play the radio as loud as he used to on our way in. There's no singing in the car; there's not as much light.

A few times, Mom has picked me up or told me to drive myself, because my dad has gotten called back down to the station for more "light questioning." Every single time, it makes me sick to my stomach.

I know where he was that night. He went to the store, and then he came home. I know I was out; I know Mom and Tucker were sleeping. But I *know* where he was. And it wasn't with Willa. It wasn't doing something terrible. He was just being Dad. Sweet, angelic, good ol' Dad.

I need to know who the eyewitness is. I need a quick word. Or two. But the cops won't say who it is. They are protecting the person who is single-handedly ruining my dad's life.

I'm walking to chemistry in a fog when Shelly nudges me.

"Oh, hey, Shell," I say.

"Hey," she says. She looks nervous.

"What's up?"

She pauses for a moment then hands me her phone. I look down at the headline staring back at me.

Tilden Teacher Questioned In Missing Persons Case, reads the cover story of the *Tilden Post.* My eyes scan the next few sentences before I can't read any more. I hand the phone back to her.

"Is everything okay?" she asks. I nod, trying like hell to hold the bile back that's building in my throat. I spin on my heel and head in the direction of the history wing.

"Mare?" Shelly asks. I stick a hand up and wave, but I can't bring myself to say anything. I know I'm going to be late to chem, and Dad has warned me that he won't write me tardy passes.

"Get your ass to class, and you won't need a pass," was his favorite saying ever when I first started high school. He stood true to his word, too. He's never, ever given me a pass.

I pop my head into his classroom, but to my surprise, he's not there. Instead, a short, plump woman with horribly dyed red hair is at the front of the room, trying desperately to get the kids' attention. My heart is pounding in my throat.

"Yo, where's Mr. P?" one kid asks. I feel my stomach flip.

"Did you not see the news?" another says, chucking

his phone to the first kid. The first kid scans the headline and then chucks the phone back.

"Damn," he whispers. Suddenly, the whispers grow louder and louder until they are completely deafening.

"Willa's brother saw him at the grocery store," says another classmate that I'd like to deck in the fucking face.

Willa's brother, eh?

The tardy bell rings, and I'm the last one in the hallway. I yank my phone from my backpack.

Where are you?

I wait, but there's no answer. I text him again.

Dad?

No answer. I enter Mom's number.

Dad's not in class. Do you know where he is?

Those three little dots are enough to give me a freaking heart attack.

Why aren't you in class?

MOM. WHERE IS DAD?

I'm coming to pick you up. Head down to the office.

I wait nervously on the bench outside Principal Pickett's office. My backpack is so freaking heavy because I carry all of my textbooks that, even sitting down, it's digging into my shoulders. I'm gnawing on my thumbnail when I see Mom's car pull up outside. She walks inside, nods at me, and then walks into the office to sign me out. As she's walking out, Principal Pickett is trailing behind her.

"Sorry about this, Caroline," he says to Mom. She rolls her eyes and spins around to him.

"If you're sorry, then why don't you stick up for the best teacher your school has ever had, rather than let the damn school board have all the control?" she asks him, hand on her hip. She nods at me to follow her out, and I do, unaware of how to acknowledge my principal whom my mom just verbally bitch-slapped.

We get in the car, and I think this is the first time I'm not anxious over missing a class. I couldn't give two shits about chemistry right now. The swirling storm in my stomach is taking precedence, clouding my judgment, and making everything else in my life non-consequential.

"Where is he?" I ask. Her hands are gripped tight on the steering wheel as she drives. She's staring straight ahead, not even blinking.

"The county has placed him on administrative leave," she says, turning to me for a moment, "pending the investigation."

My throat feels like it's on fire.

"What? How can they do that when he hasn't been formally charged with anything?" I ask. Most of my criminal knowledge comes from watching entirely too many episodes of *Law and Order: SVU,* but it's taught me a thing or two.

"The school board is separate from the police," Mom says, "and they feel that because of Dad's 'involvement' in the case, it doesn't look good to have him still teaching in the school."

I feel the blood in my body start to boil. I'm seeing red. I want to hurt someone, cause them actual, physical pain. The rest of the school is still reeling over Willa's disappearance. Search parties have been going out weekly, posters are everywhere, and her face is all over every social media network.

But for me, now, this case isn't even about Willa. And I'm angry about that, too. I should be able to worry for her safety, join my classmates in solidarity as we post signs that say "Bring Willa Home." But I can't. Because now it's about Dad.

I'M LYING on the couch that evening, Mom next to me, flipping through the newspaper, and Tucker on the floor, scrolling through his phone. Dad's in his study, trying to finish up the sub plans that the stupid county doesn't deserve from him, but he says he can't leave his kids hanging.

Lori Decklan, a long-time Long Island news fixture, pops up on the screen.

"We have an interesting development tonight in the Willa Mills case, the fourteen-year-old Tilden resident who went missing just two weeks ago. Authorities say they have no suspects yet, but they do have a person of interest," Lori says. I like Lori. She's a staple for me; she means home. But right now, I want to reach through the screen and slap the curl right out of her hair. "Chuck Ford joins us from the Tilden Police Station."

"Thank you, Lori," Chuck says. Chuck is new to Long Island news. He's not even from here. He doesn't even know what the fuck he's talking about. Shut up, Chuck. "We're live in front of the Tilden Police Station, where just moments ago, Detective Eric Robinson announced a person of interest in the case."

The screen jumps over to the earlier press conference, which, thank God, we missed watching live. I hear the stairs creak as Dad slowly makes his way down into the living room, his eyes wide as he stares at the television.

"We have an eyewitness that has placed a dark-colored SUV speeding off from the scene of the crime," says Detective Robinson, who I'd also like to nut-punch. Him, along with the mysterious eyewitness, who I know from the non-stop gossiping is likely Wyatt Mills. "We do have a person of interest that drives a similar vehicle and was an acquaintance of Miss Mills. We are not releasing that person's name at this time; however, citizens are encouraged to contact the crime help line with any information regarding Miss Mills or the SUV spotted in the Migley Market parking lot on the evening of December 23rd."

The camera switches back to Chuck.

"While authorities are not publicly sharing the name of the person of interest, there is much public speculation regarding a teacher at Tilden High School, Joe Porter."

The camera flashes over to an earlier interview with Chuck on school grounds. The woman he's interviewing is short and stout, and I've never seen her a day in my life.

"Do you know her, Dad?" I ask. He shakes his head.

"It's really unnerving to know that a teacher at my children's school could be capable of something so terrible. I'm glad the county finally did the right thing and put him on leave."

This woman doesn't know my father. Why the fuck are they even interviewing her?

The screen then flashes to a student who I recognize, Craig Chasey.

"Mr. P is a really cool teacher," he says. *Thank you, Craig Chasey.* "It's hard to believe he could be involved with something like this, but you never know, I guess."

Okay, fuck *you*, Craig Chasey.

Chuck takes the microphone back.

"Tilden County Public Schools did issue a statement last week when Mr. Porter was officially put on leave, saying that 'We find it's in the best interest for the safety of our students and staff to place Mr. Porter on adminis-trative leave until the case is resolved. We are working diligently with the Tilden Police Department to offer any help or insight we may have for the disappearance of Willa Mills.'"

I see tears forming in Mom's eyes.

"I guess I'll go call the lawyer," Dad says, his voice hushed as he walks back up the stairs. Tucker's staring at me, wide-eyed, waiting for me to say something.

But all I would be able to do right now is scream. I grab my hat and coat off the rack and walk outside. I walk down the street, secretly hoping to run into someone ignorant enough to say something to me so I can have my release. But I don't see anyone. I just see cold, bleak streets, empty, free of anyone willing to give my family a fucking break. Everything is a shade of red right now for me, and I feel my hands involuntarily balling into fists.

Goddamn you, Wyatt Mills.

You don't fuck with the Porters and get away with it.

9

WYATT

I hop up from the floor mat where I just finished doing an ab workout, and I see the same woman staring at me from the mirror. I'm pretty sure she's been following me the entire time I've been working out, and I've seen her lift her phone a few times and point it in my direction. I smile and shake my head as I dab myself with my towel and make my way up to the showers.

"Hey, man," Nate says as I walk into the locker room.

"'Sup, Nate," I say as I open up the combination lock. Our office building has a huge gym on the bottom three floors. Nate and I pretty much work out before work every day.

"So, the Landry people are comin' in today?" he asks, washing his hands at the sink.

"Yep," I say. I've been prepping for the meeting since the day I set my sights on nabbing them as a client. Landry is one of the biggest hotel chains in the world, and their business could be life-changing for Caldell.

"You ready?" he asks. I smile.

"Always, baby," I say, holding my arms out as I smile. He laughs and shakes his head.

"I saw that chick take your picture today while you were on the rower," he says. I nod and smile.

"Yeah, I saw her too."

"Why don't you get her number?" he asks. I shrug as I walk past him and turn the shower on.

"Still hung up on your little Florida fling?" he asks. My spine goes straight. I told Nate that I had a hot hookup when I went down to Florida. Told him it was some girl at the alumni dinner—which isn't totally false.

"No," I say, feeling myself grow more serious. "I'm just busy."

"Shit," Nate scoffs. "No one's too busy for some pussy, bro." I shake my head and get in the shower. "I'll see you at the office. That new coordinator starts today, so if you have time between your meetings, pop by and meet her."

My jaw locks behind the shower curtain, and I feel my entire body tense up. I put my hands up against the shower wall and drop my head.

Fuck.

The biggest client of my professional career and the best lay of my life in the same damn day. I did this to myself, though.

I shower quickly and get myself dressed. I'm wearing my best suit today, my light-gray one, and the seafoam green tie that Mom says "makes my eyes and skin pop."

When I woke up this morning, I was ready to rock. I was ready to sweep Landry off their feet, make them swoon, become their number-one guy here at the agency. But now, I'm practically shaking in my dress shoes as the elevator climbs to the seventieth floor, all because of Maryn Porter.

The elevator dings as the doors open into our grand lobby, and I kick myself into gear. I nod at Priscilla at the front desk, say hello to anyone else I pass, and swiftly make my way into my office. I need to collect myself and figure out how to avoid Maryn until after the meeting with Landry.

I'm sitting at my computer, running through my slides and notes for the millionth time, when Nate pops his head in.

"Hey, man, you almost ready?" he asks. I let out a long breath and nod.

"Yeah, man," I say.

"Cool," he says. "Before you head down, I want you to meet someone."

Before I can look up, he's waving someone in.

Goddammit, It's her.

She's dressed in a tight black skirt and a matching blazer with a polka-dot shirt poking out from the collar. She's wearing black high heels and has her long, blonde hair pulled back into a ponytail. It takes me a second before I realize that I'm scouring her with my eyes and haven't yet "introduced" myself. I clear my throat and walk around from behind my desk. I hold out my hand.

"This is Maryn Porter, the new coordinator," Nate says. She's staring at me, but she doesn't look surprised. She knew I worked here. Yet, she still took the job. She narrows her eyes a bit then sticks out her hand.

"Maryn," I say, "it's nice to meet you." A twinge of a smile tugs on her lips before fading away.

"Thank you, I'm glad to be here," she says with her

voice, but her eyes are saying "Fuck you"—and not in the good kind of way.

"Wyatt, here, just got promoted to Vice President a few weeks ago," Nate says. "He's brought in some of our biggest clients, including Landry hotels, who he's getting ready to meet with today."

Her eyes flash back to mine and instantly grow colder. Although, the Landry name did seem to impress her the slightest bit.

"Wow," she says with a nod.

"You'll be working with Wyatt's team a good deal," Nate says, and I watch her eyes grow wide again. "Might be traveling a few times a year to some of our clients."

She nods slowly, still staring directly at me. Yikes.

"Well, good luck today," she says as they turn to walk out of my office. "Hopefully, you can nail it."

Nate doesn't catch on, but what she's really saying is, "I sort of hope you crash and burn." And I don't know why, but it feels like a challenge. It gets me hot and bothered in the best fucking way. Why the *fuck* did I do this to myself?

"Well, good luck, Wyatt. Knock 'em dead," Nate says, leading her out of my office. My head drops, and I rub the back of my neck. The biggest fucking hotel chain in the world, and my most stressful encounter today will be with the blonde in the pencil skirt.

THE MEETING with Landry goes amazing. It doesn't take me long before I'm back in the game, feeling like my normal self. I'm not arrogant, but I know that I'm good at my job. And I don't feel guilty about climbing to the top quicker than most, because I know I deserve it. After everything I've been through, after everything my family has been through, and after all the work I've put into this, I deserve it.

I'll be heading out to Chicago in a few weeks to present the official communications plans at Landry's headquarters. It's going to be a big deal. Our CEO is coming with us, and so is Nate. It's gonna be another doozy, another career-defining moment for me. But I know I've got it.

I sit back in my seat, chucking my Yankees ball up and down again.

"Heard you killed it as usual," Nate says as he takes a seat across from me.

I smile and nod.

"Yeah, man. I'm really excited," he says. "That's awesome. This is huge. Seriously."

I nod.

"So, I have a meeting with Sellman this afternoon. Hope you don't mind, but I set up some time for you to meet with Maryn and give her the lowdown on some of your clients. She'll be going to Chicago with us, so I figured it would be good to show her the ropes before that. She's in training till this afternoon, then she knows to come here."

I nod slowly—too slow. I clear my throat.

"Uh, yeah, that should be fine. I can clear my schedule."

"No need; Priscilla already checked it and penciled her in. She's yours from four to five," Nate says, standing up from the chair and walking toward the door. "I think she's gonna do really well here. Good choice."

I fall back against my chair and rub my temples.

She's so fucking sexy. And smart. And I'm the most masochistic son of a bitch in the world for bringing her here. It's going to be torturous. But besides my unwavering attraction to her, there's still something inside of me that feels like I owe her. Like I should do something to make her life better.

The rest of the day goes by pretty slowly. I have no other meetings and am just catching up on some things. I've had the occasional visitor pop in to congratulate me on Landry, including Rex, Nate's dad and the CEO of Caldell.

"The best damn decision I've ever made in my professional career was hiring you, kid," he says, popping a handful of nuts into his mouth as he stands in my office doorway. He points a finger to me. "Proud of you, kid." I nod.

"Thank you, sir."

"We'll be celebrating big in Chicago," he says as he makes his way down the hall. I swallow. Chicago. Maryn. I look at the clock. It's 3:59. And wouldn't you know it, she appears, right on time.

"Hey," I say, standing up from my desk.

"Hello," she says. I walk around to greet her and point her to the couches at the back corner of my office.

"Please, have a seat, make yourself comfortable," I say. I shut the door behind her, then take a seat on the chair across from her.

She sits down and delicately crosses one leg over the other. She reaches into her bag and pulls out a notebook and a pen and sets them on her lap. Then, she lifts those big blue eyes to me, and I feel my stomach flip.

"So, how's your first day going?" I ask, leaning back

in the chair and flipping my jacket open a bit, trying to look comfortable.

"Look," she says, pulling her blazer down, "let's not do this. I appreciate you putting in the final word, but I could have gotten this job on my own."

I shoot an eyebrow up.

"That's sort of like a 'thank you,' but not really," I say with a half-smile. Her lips press into a hard line.

"It's definitely not a 'thank you.' I deserve this job, and I could have gotten it without you," she says. I nod.

"That's true. You were on the top of the list without my input," I say.

"I didn't take this job to be closer to you," she says, and her boldness makes me twitch. "I took it *in spite* of you. I took it because I want you to regret the strings you pulled, asking for me to be here, knowing how much I loathe you."

I know she's serious, but I can't help but smile at her fiery words. I narrow my eyes at her.

"Pretty bold to talk to a VP that way," I say. She scoffs.

"I don't give a damn what your title is. You are 100% *not* my manager," she says, crossing her arms over her chest in a way that pushes her breasts up and gives me a straight shot of her cleavage. I swallow.

"You're right," I say, leaning forward a bit. "But we will be working together very closely on a lot of projects." To my surprise, she mirrors my actions and leans forward.

"If you think I will ever be working as closely with you as I did in Florida, you are sadly, sadly mistaken," she says, her voice just above a whisper. "I might work with you now, but I still absolutely hate you, Wyatt Mills."

I sit back in my chair and look her up and down.

"So you've said," I say with a smirk.

"You destroyed my family, me, for years," she says, standing up from the couch. "We lost everything. Florida was a mishap that will not happen again. But what will happen is that you will regret the moment you plucked my resume off your desk. I'm not here to make nice, Wyatt. I'm here to get even."

She stalks over to the door, not even waiting to see if there's anything else for us to discuss. I should be pissed. I should be reporting her to Nate. But I won't. Because I wanted this. I wanted her to be here. I want her again— body, mind, soul. I want her to not fucking hate me.

"Well, then," I say, just as she's opening the door, "guess I'll see you in Chicago."

She turns to me slowly.

"What's in Chicago?" she asks.

"Landry headquarters," I say. "It'll be your first business trip."

She sighs and closes the door behind her.

Don't worry, Miss Porter. I'll be a total gentleman.

Unless you don't want me to.

10

MARYN

I get home and slam the apartment door shut, and within a moment, Ellie is emerging from her bedroom. We got *so* lucky. We got a great deal on this place, and Ellie's dad paid a little extra for them to let us move in early. I'm still not unpacked, but I am loving being in the city. It's loud here, and I love it.

"Well, I was gonna ask you how your first day went, but—"

"Ugh," I say, throwing my bag down on the couch and kicking off my pumps. I walk to the fridge and pluck a bottle of wine from the top of it. I slam a glass down on the counter in front of me and fill 'er up.

"That good, huh?" Ellie says. I guzzle the wine like it's water before stalking back over and plopping on the couch.

"He's going to make my life hell," I say.

"Why? Did he say something? Is he harassing you?" she asks. I sigh.

"No."

"Well, what did he say?"

"He welcomed me to the company," I say. She raises her eyebrows.

"Well, what did he *do?*" she asks. I sigh again.

"Nothing, I guess. He's just...*there.*" She smiles, which gets me all fired up. "What? There's nothing funny about this."

"Oh, nothing," she says. "It's just that you hate him a lot. But you also want to get in his pants again."

"*What?*" I say, shock all over my face. She giggles as she walks to the kitchen.

"I'm telling you, Mare, that right there," she says, pointing to my face, "is the face of a sexually frustrated woman."

"No. No fucking way. I despise him," I say. She crosses her arms and purses her lips out.

"Did you despise him when he was screwing you silly?"

I make a gagging noise.

"Can we please not use the term 'screwing you silly?'" I ask. "And yeah. I did hate him. Every second of it." I pause. "Except for maybe the very end," I add sheepishly.

She chuckles.

"This is me you're talking to, not Keely. So you can be honest about it. It doesn't make ya weak, kid," she says. "It's okay if, over time, you don't hate him as much."

She goes back into her room as I collapse back against the couch.

AFTER THE FIRST few weeks on the job, I'm actually really liking it. So far, I haven't run into Wyatt a whole lot; I can see his office from my cubicle, so I know exactly what times to avoid the kitchen so that we don't get coffee at the same time. We make eye contact every so often, but for the most part, that's been the extent of our conversation.

I really like Nate. As far as managers go—and as far as someone who's never had a manager thinks—he's pretty cool. He gives me a lot of work, but lets me run with it without breathing down my neck. I'm making friends with a lot of my other coworkers, too, which is something that Wyatt seems to be not so fond of. He's broken up a few pow-wows at my desk and seems to have a scowl on his face when he walks by and sees someone talking to me. It gives me more satisfaction than I care to admit.

I think Wyatt and I have done a good job of not letting on that we knew each other in a past life. No one seems to suspect anything, and due to our lack of inter-acting, I don't see that being an issue in the future.

I'm sitting at my desk, working on a press release, when Nate walks by and taps on my cube.

"Hey, do you have a minute for a quick meeting in Wyatt's office?" he asks. I hop up and grab my notebook.

"Sure," I say.

When we get in, Wyatt and Nate are making small talk, talking about the Yankees and some new workout class Nate's been taking. Finally, we all sit down on the leather couches. Nate hands us each a piece of paper.

"So, I just wanted to go over the itinerary for Chica-go," he says. I clear my throat as I scan the sheet. "So, you guys will leave Monday, if that works." I look up to Nate.

"You're not coming?" I ask. He shakes his head.

"Unfortunately, I got called into another big meeting next week with one of our other bigger clients. Don't worry, though. Wyatt, here, will show you the ropes and take good care of you." I nod. For fuck's sake.

"Rex is going out there a little bit early," Nate says. "Your guys' flight will land around seven p.m. on Monday, and you can meet Rex for a late dinner to go over everything for the meeting Tuesday." I'm still getting used to the fact that Nate calls his dad by his first name; I guess it would be weird for a thirty-something-year-old man to walk around the halls asking for his daddy, though.

Wyatt's eyes flash up to me, then to Nate, and he nods.

"Sounds good."

"So, I know you're probably more than ready, but Maryn, if Wyatt needs any help with any of the materials this week, think you can help him out?"

I nod.

"Absolutely," I say, trying to fight back the bile in my throat.

"I might just have you take a look at everything, just to get a second pair of eyes on it," he says.

I nod.

"Great, I'll send that to you this afternoon."

WHEN I GET BACK to my desk, I open a group text.

We're on the same freakin flight next week.

Who? Keely asks. *Oh, wait, you and Wy-guy?*

Yes. And don't give him pet names. We hate him, remember?

Oh, yeah, sorry.

Ha, Ellie chimes in. *You're losing that battle, honey.*

Oh, is she now? Keely asks.

Hell yeah. She wants the D. AGAIN, Ellie says. I roll my eyes.

Ok, first of all, fuck you both. Second of all. NO. I don't. I can't. He RUINED our lives. I hate him.

Ellie sends a GIF of a girl rolling her eyes.

Fine. Then get your butt to Chicago and make him regret the very minute he set his sights on your family.

I take in a breath. *Hope you're ready for me, Mr. Mills.*

I GET to the airport extra early, check in early, and sit by myself in a far corner of the waiting area for the flight, hoping to God I don't have to see him. At least, not yet. I'm successful until I get on the plane and see him there, in first class, already boarded and comfy cozy. We make eye contact, and he nods at me. I make something similar to a gag noise then walk by him, shuffling my way back to the common folk.

When we land, I take my time getting off, giving him plenty of time to get off ahead of me. I wait for my baggage and head out to the front of the airport to wait for a cab.

"Took ya long enough," I hear his cool voice say, and my spine goes straight. Fuck me.

"Why are you still here?" I ask.

"Thought we could cab share. Ya know, save the company a few dollars," he says. He sticks his hand out, and a cab pulls around.

"I'd rather just pay for my own out of my own pocket," I say. He laughs as he bends down to grab my bag.

"Come on, now," he says, putting both of our bags in the trunk. "Let's be grownups."

I roll my eyes and get in the cab. The whole ride to the hotel, I stare out the window, trying to take in the sights and sounds of Chicago and ignore the enemy next to me.

"Ever been to Chi-town?" he asks. I shake my head.

"Nope," I say, without looking at him.

We ride the rest of the way in silence. He pays for the cab, and then we make our way inside to the front desk. We get our room keys and head to the elevators. I'm on the 18th floor, and he's on the 28th. Phew. Ten whole floors between us. Last time I was in a hotel with him... There cannot—*will* not—be a repeat of last time.

We ride up in silence, but I can feel his eyes on me.

"You and I," he says, and I look at him, "are clearly not going to be friends."

I laugh.

"Clearly."

"Can we just be civil?" he asks. I sigh, my eyes dropping to the floor then searching the buttons, hoping for eighteen.

"If I had taken everything from you, would you want to be civil?" I ask him just as the elevator doors open. I walk off and turn back to him.

"I thought he did," he says.

"What?" I say.

"Your father. I thought he *did* take everything from me."

The doors close, and I'm standing in the hallway with my jaw at the ground.

I throw my things on my bed and look around the room. I text my parents to let them know I've landed safely and then do a re-con of my appearance in the mirror. I might be in the middle of a battle with Wyatt, but I need to cool my jets for this dinner. Rex Calloway is the CEO of our company. He and Rick Wadell—hence, Cal-Dell—started the company back in the 80's from Rick's parents' basement. And now they're here. Rick passed away a few years back, according to the "About Us" pamphlet I got at my orientation. Rex runs it now, with Nate and, apparently, Wyatt following behind him.

It's time to turn on the charm, show Mr. Calloway why I'm supposed to be here. That one day, maybe I'll be following right along behind him, too.

I ride the elevator back down to the lobby and walk across to the restaurant where we're meeting.

Rex is a big man. He rivals Wyatt in height. He's got salt-and-pepper hair, electric-blue eyes, and he's always tan, just as you'd expect someone who goes to the Bahamas four or five times a year to be. He always smells good, and as far as CEOs go, he's actually pretty involved with his company. He shows his face a lot.

When I walk toward him, Wyatt's already sitting down next to him, which irks me. I'm early, but Wyatt was earlier.

They both stand to greet me and shake my hand.

"Welcome, Maryn," Rex says, holding his hand out for me to take a seat. "How was the flight?"

"Fine," I say with a warm smile. "Chicago seems great."

He smiles.

"It's great," he says. "So, I'm just walking Wyatt through our schedule. We will have lunch tomorrow with a few of the executives and then give our presentation after that. Then, hopefully, we will be celebrating with dinner and drinks after!"

I smile and nod.

"That sounds great!" I say.

"Great," Rex says. The rest of lunch is weird for me. Wyatt and Rex are discussing the Landry deal and a bunch of other ones I haven't been around long enough to know about. I know I'm entry-level, but I'm soaking this all in. I'm remembering names and companies to research later. I *will* be a pro. Finally, Rex calls the waiter over to pay the bill, and I know I'm almost free.

I say goodbye with a sweet smile on my face then briskly walk to the elevator. I hit the button to close the doors before Wyatt is even out of the restaurant. I let myself into my room and shut the door, then let out a long breath. Phew. I did it. I made it to my hotel room without Wyatt Mills.

I take a long, hot shower, blow-dry my hair, and lay my clothes out for the next day. I hop on the bed and turn on *Golden Girls.* No one gets me quite like Sophia.

As I'm chowing down on another airport cookie, my cell vibrates. I grab it and see a message from an unknown number.

I made some last-minute changes to a few of my slides. Any chance you can review them?

How the hell does he have my number?

How do you have my number?

Nate gave it to me before we left in case we wanted to hook up while we were here.

I swallow as my eyes grow wide.

For dinner or anything, after the meeting.

Nice save.

Oh. Yeah, that's fine. Just send them over.

Actually, I sort of want to run through them. Do you mind being my audience?

I swallow again. No, no, Mr. Mills. Nice try.

I think for a moment, knowing that the disappearing and reappearing dots on his screen are probably driving him mad.

I remind myself that I hate him.

I don't want him.

This will be easy. Just run through the slides and leave.

He ruined me; he ruined my dad; he ruined my family. It's all because of him.

This will be easy.

Okay. Send me your room number.

807.

Be up in a few.

I go to the mirror and fluff my hair some and change into yoga pants and a t-shirt. I know he's one of the partners at my job, but I'm certainly not dressing up for him. And aside from that, he's already seen me naked.

I go to walk out of my room and pause. I turn back to the mirror and put on a few flicks of mascara.

You never know who you might see roaming the halls.

I feel bubbles in my stomach as I ride the elevator up the ten floors, tapping my foot anxiously. I find 807 and knock. He answers, and my insides melt.

He's got on baggy gray sweatpants and a plain white t-shirt that's tight around his muscles. His bright-green eyes are extra bright tonight, which I find *extra* annoying.

"Hey," he says, standing back to let me in. "Thanks for coming up."

I nod and breeze by him. His room is bigger than mine, with a couch in the corner and a desk where he's got his laptop and notes all set up. I'll give it to him: he's a hard worker. And as much as it pains me to admit it, he deserves his position, too.

"So," I say, sitting on the couch, "what do we got?"

"Okay," he says, scurrying over to the desk to unplug his computer. He perches it on the dresser next to him, clears his throat, and begins his presentation. The first few slides are the same as they were before. I nod along with him, having almost memorized them from how many times I reviewed them. I checked them up and down, side to side, one million times, needing them to be perfect—for the Landry account, for Rex, for the company, for me. Maybe a teeny, tiny bit for Wyatt.

"Okay, now here's where I changed it up a bit," he says. He clears his throat again. "Landry has over 6,000 hotels spanning the globe. That's 6,000 locations that some people have never seen. That's 6,000 places to host a business retreat, a wedding, a 50th anniversary trip. Six thousand opportunities to show people all around the world the time of their life," he says. He goes on, and I don't even realize I'm gaping at him. The smoothness with which he presents, the confidence he exudes, makes me really fucking turned on.

He finishes the last slide and looks up at me.

"What do you think about that last part? Do you think it's—"

"It's perfect," I say. His eyes widen. "It's really fucking good. Don't change anything. They will love it."

He nods and closes his computer.

"Thanks for listening and coming up here. I know it's late, but I just really want this to go well," he says, and his moment of vulnerability catches me off guard. I stand up from the couch and start heading for the door. He follows behind me, rubbing the back of his neck.

"You're gonna kill it tomorrow," I say. "They are going to be so happy they signed this contract."

And I hate how nice I'm being. How civil. But I think about what he said when those elevator doors closed.

Your father. I thought he did take everything.

He puts his hand on the door handle and looks down at me.

"You're doing a really great job, Maryn. You're a really good fit here," he says. His eyes are moving back and forth between mine. I see them drop down to my lips, and I feel my tongue jut out to wet them. Suddenly, breathing feels a little bit harder as I start to stare at him. And then I can't stop.

I step up onto my tip-toes and press my lips against his, sucking his bottom lip into my mouth. I sweep my tongue into his for a brief moment, then come back down to my feet, down to Earth, and step back. I'm staring at him now, waiting for his next move. He takes a step closer to me so that my back is flush up against the door.

"I'm not sure what you want from me, Maryn," he whispers, "but whatever it is, you're gonna have to lead the way. I know what I want, but I'm not taking anything else from you."

It's a sweet gesture, but it also sort of pisses me off that he thinks he's being such a gentleman, protecting my feelings, not taking advantage of me. Well, that's fine. Because I'll just take advantage of *him.*

I kiss him again, pushing him further into his room

until we reach the couch again. I slam him down and straddle him, and before I know it, he has my shirt off over my head. Ha, that was fast. He's unhooking my bra as I'm tugging at his t-shirt, and I can feel him hardening under his sweatpants. I kiss his jawline and nibble at his neck. My breasts spring free from my bra as he tosses it to the floor, and he takes me into his mouth so slowly it hurts. He tugs at my nipples gently with his teeth then pushes me back gently so he can kiss my chest and neck.

"Maryn," he says in a sort of groany whisper, "are you sure about this?"

I push him off of me and stare right into those big, green, shiny eyes of his.

"Fuck you, Wyatt," I say just as I begin grinding my groin against his. He drops his head back, exposing his neck and his Adam's apple, which my tongue gleefully trails, flicking back and forth, drawing lines. He moans again and then brings his head up.

"Yes, ma'am," he says and pushes to his feet. He sets me down and kisses me one more time before dropping to his knees in front of me. He reaches up and tugs my yogas down, taking his sweet, sweet time. He loops his thumbs into the strings of my thong and shimmies it down my legs, sending chills up and down my whole body. He throws me back against the couch and pushes my knees apart, kissing me one more time before leaving a trail of kisses headed south. He pushes my legs even farther apart then breathes softly, slowly onto my center. I tilt my head back and clutch onto the couch for dear life.

His tongue starts to work on me, and I swear he's

84

finding spots I didn't even know existed. He's pumping it in and out of me, separating me, exploring me.

"Wyatt," I moan, clutching onto the back of his head. He sucks and kisses and licks until I'm a soaking mess, then kisses his way back up my body. He kisses next to my ear and pushes my hair out of the way.

"Maryn," he whispers.

"Hmm?"

"Tell me you don't hate me," he says. I lick my lips, my center throbbing, begging for more of him.

"I do. I do hate you," I say, breathless, closing my eyes and soaking in the moment.

He stands up in front of me and pulls his pants and boxers down, and I almost forgot how impressive he is. Every single inch of him.

I reach out to touch him, but he pushes my hand away. He drops back down to his knees, his eyes trained on mine, and pushes one finger, then two fingers inside of me.

"Maryn," he says again, his voice a little more stern this time. "Tell me you don't hate me."

His fingers are moving inside of me, fast then slow, circling, then in and out, hitting that spot with every fucking move. My whole body is squirming on the couch now, like I'm having a goddamn out-of-body experience.

"No," I say again. He leans up to give my aching parts one last kiss then slowly slides his fingers out.

I know what he's doing. He's fucking teasing me.

And it's working.

He's standing in front of me, fully erect, the muscles in his body braced for action, braced for me. My heart is beating out of my chest, and my insides feel like they're ready to burst. Is it possible to die from almost having an orgasm, but then not? Can girls get blue balls? Because I'm pretty sure I have them.

I reach up and grab a hold of his shaft, and before he can pull away, I take him into my mouth. I slide my lips down once, twice, three times, fast then slow, making his legs shake as he stands in front of me. When I have him at his most vulnerable state, I stand up and spin him around, pushing him onto the couch.

I'm staring at him like he's prey—because maybe he is.

I take one step toward him then straddle him. He puts his hands on either of my hips, his head dropped back against the couch, his eyes closed.

"Maryn," he whispers, but I know I'm winning this round. I ease myself onto him slowly, taking in just the tip and watching what it does to him. The way his eyebrows knit together when he feels my warmth taking him in is almost enough to make me come without even making another move. I wrap my hand around his neck and pull him into me. I kiss his lips one more time and press mine to his ear.

"I hate you, Wyatt Mills," I say, and then I slide myself onto him, taking every inch of him inside of me, making us both moan simultaneously. "I. Hate. You," I tell him, thrusting up and down on top of him.

I can feel my wetness running down the insides of my legs and onto him.

"Jesus Christ, Maryn," he whispers, pulling me closer and burying his face in my neck. I press my hands to his chest, rocking back and forth as fast as I can, not wanting this build-up to ever end. But to my surprise, he takes over again. He somehow finds the will to move to his feet, holding me in the air as he's still inside of me.

He gently slides me off of him and brings me to the bed, turning me around so that I'm facing away from him. He moves quickly and pushes himself inside of me from behind. I'm on all fours, panting, clawing at his sheets, seeing fucking stars.

He pumps fast, then faster. And then it happens. I explode, my grip on the sheets finally loosening up.

"Fuck!" I call out as my head drops to the bed. He moans one more time, and with one more thrust, I can feel him shaking inside of me, emptying himself. He slides out of me, and we collapse onto the bed. He drapes his arm across my back, and I feel him tuck a piece of hair behind my ear.

"I can tell you something, Maryn," he whispers against it. "I certainly do not hate you."

My head is turned away from him, and in a weird mix of emotions, I suddenly feel like I

want to cry. Tears are prickling at the back of my eyes, and I clear my throat to get myself together. I lie next to him for a few minutes, collecting myself, trying to figure out how the fuck that just happened...again.

Oh, my God. I fucking just fucked Wyatt Mills again. *Fuck.*

I slide out from under his arm and scurry to find my clothes. I rush into the bathroom to clean myself up and get dressed in a hurry. I pull my hair into a messy bun and walk out. I put my hand on the door handle, but he's standing there in front of me. He has his pants on now, his bare chest taunting me, reminding me of what I've just done.

"Maryn..." he starts to say, but I open the door. I turn my head to him slightly.

"Fuck you, Wyatt," I whisper then walk out the door.

It's all I can do not to burst into tears as I ride down to my room. I know he has to be confused, because I'm confusing myself. When I lose it like that, when I take him, let him take me, it's like I can't stop. Like I'm not me, and like he's not him. We are just two people who have to have each other. And it's frustrating as hell.

11

FEBRUARY 2015- WYATT

She's been gone for six weeks. Six weeks since I've seen her. Six weeks since we've heard from her. Six weeks since any signal could be detected from her cell phone. I swear I've watched the footage of her going into that store a hundred times.

Mom hasn't slept. She wanders around the house like she's possessed. She did all of Willa's laundry then, once it was clean, began washing all of her clean clothes. She made her bed, then moved things around, then put them back in order.

She sent notes to Willa's teachers, letting them know she would be out of class indefinitely, as if they weren't already aware.

Dad...he's just angry. He sleeps all day, stays up all night. Calls the detective on our case at least three times a day, asking for updates. He won't look me in the eye. He hasn't said it, but he doesn't have to. I know there's a part of him that blames me for not keeping an eye on her.

I haven't said it, but I blame me a little bit, too.

It was a crowded night at the store. And it's Tilden. Not much happens here. But something big happened that night, and I can't take it back. I can't go back and make her wait for me to park and go in. I can't do anything about it except curse myself for being so irresponsible.

All I can do is focus on the fact that I saw that teacher there. I saw a car that looked like his speed off just a short while after he and my sister spoke.

I don't know much about him, but I can't shake this feeling. I know there's something to it. I know there's something there. There has to be.

We saw him walking into the station one day last week when we were walking out. I stopped in my tracks, giving him a stare that told him how badly I wanted to fuck him up. Dad gave him the same one, and Mom just stood there, staring down at her feet.

But the teacher, Mr. Porter, he just nodded to us, his eyes solemn, as he walked by. He didn't exactly *look* guilty, but the guilty ones never do. Mr. Porter is a tall, slender man. You can tell he loves his history books, but he's also fairly fit. Could certainly drag a teenager into a car if he wanted to.

Speaking of teenagers, I think he has some himself. His daughter is a year ahead of Willa in school. A few times, I've wondered about her. Does she know what he's done? Does she know where my sister is? I try to avoid thinking the worst about people, especially the ones I don't know. But in this case, if thinking the worst will bring Willa back, so be it. I don't owe these people anything. But the world owes me my sister.

I'm supposed to go back to Melladon in a few weeks, but the thought of leaving is making me nauseous. My professors have all granted me an extension on my semester start and are letting me come back later due to the circumstance. But how can I leave my parents like this? How can I just up and go back, not knowing if she will ever return? The answer is pretty simple. As the oldest child, and as their *only* child currently, I can't leave. So we have to find her.

I get inside from a short run and grab a bottle of water from the fridge. Dad's sitting in his big maroon recliner in front of the television, watching it with a blank expression.

"Hey, Pop," I say as I sit down on the floor near him to stretch.

"Hey," he says, eyes never leaving the T.V.

"Where's Ma?"

"At the store."

Oh, Ma. That's the other thing she keeps doing: going to the grocery store. Like whoever took Willa, or wherever she went, she will come back to Migley's Market. We're both sitting in silence, watching reruns of M*A*S*H, when Dad's phone buzzes on the chair next to him. His eyes drop down to it, and finally, the rest of his body reacts. He moves slowly to answer it—so slowly that it physically hurts me.

"Yes, hello," he says. "Yes, this is he." He pauses to nod for a few moments, his eyebrows tugging together. I hate that look on his face. It's usually one of anger, confusion, or just him wanting to be left alone. It's almost become a permanent fixture on his face for the last few weeks.

"Certainly. My wife should be home momentarily, and we will make our way down."

He hangs up the phone and calls Mom, letting her

know the detective has some updates. He tells her to get home as soon as she can.

"I want to come, Dad," I say, hopping up from the table. He doesn't say anything, just sort of grumbles and nods. I skip over a few steps as I head up to my room to shower.

I have the T.V. on in my bedroom what feels like 24/7. It kills the silence, which prevents me from having to sit and think. Sit and wonder about all the possibilities, the terrible things that could be happening—or already have happened—to my little sister.

The sounds from the T.V. drown out the unpleasantries that have taken a permanent residence in this goddamn house.

As I'm toweling off, I hear the familiar voice of the evening news anchor, Lori Decklan, a long-time Long Island fixture.

"The town of Tilden is hosting a vigil at the high school this evening in celebration of Willa Mills' sixteenth birthday. Willa went missing on the night of December 23rd when she went to the grocery store with her older brother and never returned home," Lori says.

December 23rd will live on as my least favorite day, forever.

"We're just all so broken up over this." The camera shows Principal Pickett, whom I know has probably never spoken to my sister a day in his life. I also always suspected him of being a little bit racist, but that's a different story. "Willa is such a bright soul. We just want her brought back safely and soon."

I roll my eyes.

The camera goes back to Lori.

"Police are still not releasing the name of their

person of interest, but Tilden County Public Schools put history teacher Joe Porter on administrative leave, pending his involvement in the investigation, back in January."

The camera flashes over to a man standing in front of the high school. I recognize his last name; I think his older son went to school with me. He must have a younger kid in school now.

"It's disheartening, for sure, to know that someone who works so closely with our kids could possibly be involved in this," the man says. "He should definitely be kept off of school grounds. I don't want him around my kids, that's for sure."

I don't know why, but this itty bitty pang of guilt goes through me. I pull on a sweatshirt and head downstairs.

I've memorized almost every detail about the inside of the police station at this point, which is something I thought I'd never say.

They have these metal chairs with the scratchiest fabric I've ever touched stretched across them. There's one on the very end of the row that doesn't match the others, and it really bothers me.

There's a small section of four desks directly across from the sitting area, but I only ever see one woman, Rochel, at her desk when we come. She answers all the phones and is the assistant to Detective Robinson.

The wall behind us is lined with offices, which, again, are normally empty whenever we come. I suspect the detectives who work in them aren't able to spend a ton of time behind a desk.

Finally, Detective Robinson's door opens.

"Hi, folks," he says, "thanks for coming back in."

My dad's face lightens a little bit when he sees Detective Robinson. So far, he's the only person throughout all of this who has really dug deep for us. He's our main advocate. He takes every detail seriously.

We sit down across from his desk in his cramped office as he sits down and folds his hands on his desk.

"I have some questions concerning Willa," he says, opening a folder. "Can you tell me, again, what she was wearing that night?"

My parents' eyes both find me immediately. I swallow.

"She was wearing gray Tilden High sweatpants and a purple Tilden sweatshirt," I say. She had a matching purple headband in her hair."

Detective Robinson nods. He lifts up a piece of paper and slides out a plastic bag. In it, is a purple headband. Willa's purple headband. My mom gasps. My dad's eyebrows knit together again. And I feel like I'm going to throw up.

"Where did you find this?" Mom asks, her chin quivering.

"One of our patrols picked it up just outside of Stone Creek Park," Detective Robinson says. "It was located in a wooded area. Our search team has deployed, but nothing has come up yet."

Mom keeps gasping, clutching her hands to her chest as she stares down at it.

"It's important to keep your head up and your eyes open, guys," Detective Robinson says. "I know it's hard. But this has been examined," he says, lifting the plastic bag, "and we're hoping to get the results back soon. Just keep your eyes peeled for her. Keep the faith."

My parents stand up and shake Detective Robinson's

hand. I nod in his direction, but my hands are so clammy that I don't even offer him one.

"Oh, and one more thing," he says. "We think it might be a good time for you to speak to the press, if you are comfortable. It might be a good time to ask for the public's help, get more people involved. Would any of you be okay with that?"

Mom looks to Dad, who looks at the ground. We all wait a beat, and then I step forward.

"I will," I say. Detective Robinson waits for my parents to nod in approval then excuses himself to call some contacts. We wait on the scratchy seats again, then he returns a few minutes later.

A man is following him, and I can see he has some sort of Tilden Police badge on.

"This is Connor Maynes, our public relations specialist," Detective Robinson says. I nod.

"Hi there," Connor says. "We have a few news crews gathering out on the steps right now. So, what we want to do is really let the public know what you've been dealing with. Really let them see how tough it's been. Show them how bad you want Willa home," he says. I grow inexplicably angry.

"We *do* want her home," I say. This isn't some fucking game.

"Right, right, of course. Time to let them know," he says with this weird smile that makes me want to throttle him into the desks behind us. A few more minutes pass, and Connor walks us out to the front door. I can see what looks like ten news crews standing on the steps, reporters with microphones in hand, cameras all set up and ready. I swallow. *This is for you, Willa.*

Connor walks us outside and leads us to the podium.

He says a few brief words about the "devastated Mills family" and introduces me.

I step up to the podium, my parents at my sides. I take a breath and look up.

"My sister, Willa, has been missing for over forty days. Forty days without her. Forty days since I watched her walk into that grocery store and never come back out of the front door. We haven't given up, and we're asking you not to, either. If you see anything, remember anything from that night, please contact the Tilden Police Department. Our family is asking—*begging*—for your help," I say. I can barely see from all the bright lights in my eyes. "If you have my sister," I say, staring directly into the lens of one of the cameras, "please just bring her home to us."

I step back slightly, and a wave of reporters' hands go up. Connor steps over and nods to me, taking my place at the podium to field them, most of which he answers with, "I'm not at liberty to share that information at this time."

We ride home in complete silence.

Who knew that a simple purple headband could bring such a feeling of impending doom.

My parents have been asleep for a few hours now, but I know I won't be sleeping tonight. I'm sitting on the porch, staring up at the sky, freezing my ass off. Looking for a goddamn answer. Tilden is asleep right now. People are moving on with their lives while I'm stuck on this fucking treadmill of not knowing shit.

But as I'm staring up, something catches my eye. A small, slender figure is making its way down the sidewalk. Its pace quickens, and I push myself up to my feet. This is weird.

It's hooded, wearing dark clothes.

But it's short and thin.

Like a teenaged girl.

Like my sister.

I hold my breath and take a step down. I narrow my eyes, trying to make out her curls from under her hood, or the point of her nose, the tiny mole on her left cheek. Anything to let me know it's her.

"Willa?" I whisper. The figure stops at our front walk. She reaches up and tugs off her hood, and my stomach sinks.

It's not Willa.

"You," the girl says, her eyes narrowed in the dim streetlight.

"Can I...can I help you?" I ask.

The girl snorts.

"You could have helped me a few weeks ago by keeping your goddamn mouth shut," she says. I widen my eyes.

I know who she is.

She's his daughter.

"Excuse me?"

"You could have kept your mouth shut before you went and destroyed an innocent man," she says. I swallow. "Fuck you, Wyatt Mills."

For a moment, I almost felt guilty. But now, I'm just more angry.

I take a step closer to her, but to my surprise, she doesn't even flinch.

"Careful, girl. Those are some fightin' words."

I see her eyes flare with anger.

"I know your family is hurting," she says, "and if I could, I'd bring Willa back for your parents. But you. You've destroyed a whole other family, and you don't even realize it. So, call my words what you want, but trust me when I say I've never meant something more."

Then, I watch as Maryn Porter turns around and walks back down the street, disappearing into the dark.

12

WYATT

I feel like I'm in middle school, getting rejected for the third time by Sierra Davis when I asked her to the eighth grade formal.

I'm lying in my hotel bed, a grown-ass man, feeling completely left for dead by a girl five years my junior, technically my subordinate at work, who I just slept with...*again.*

At first, the whole "I hate you" thing felt like a game. It was one I wanted to play. I wanted to hear her say it while I was inside of her, coaxing that lie from her lips. But now, I want to change her mind. I want her to stop saying it. And I want her to keep winding up in my bed. When she left my room tonight, I felt guilty, like I'd done something to purposefully hurt her. I know I didn't; I explicitly told her that I wouldn't be making the moves until she made it clear that she wanted me to.

I think her jumping my bones counted as her making it clear.

So, why I'm sitting here like a giant pussy now that she's gone is beyond me. It was that look in her eyes, I think. That look that told me that there's at least a part of her that really does *hate* me.

The next morning, I wake up groggily at the crack of dawn to head down to the hotel gym before our meeting today. I've got to run it out.

I hop on the treadmill, wearing a t-shirt with the sleeves cut off and a pair of basketball shorts. J. Cole is blasting through my headphones—entirely too loud, I know—as I start picking up the speed. But I almost fly off the damn end of it when I see her walking ahead of me down toward the yoga room.

I cut my run insanely short, hopping off and pretending like I'm going to take a leak. I make my way into the yoga room when I see her in the corner, legs spread in front of her as she bends toward them to stretch.

The silhouette of her body in those tight leggings and tight, tight little tank top make me hard behind my shorts. Unbelievable. I just fucking had her mere hours ago. My dick is a traitor.

I pause for a moment, watching her steady her breathing as she stretches. Then, I make my way over to her and nudge her foot with mine.

"Didn't know you worked out," I say, which is a fucking lie. I've seen her naked. You don't get those abs and that ass from sitting around eating Nutella all day.

She doesn't say anything, just rolls her eyes and closes them again.

"If you don't mind," she says, "I'm trying to control my breathing, get centered." Then her big blue eyes flash open and find me. "Trying not to tear off anyone's head today."

I can't help but smile. She's so damn feisty. Just as

I'm about to take a seat next to her, she pushes herself to her feet. Her bare arms and chest are glistening in sweat, and I lick my lips at the sight of her.

She rolls up the yoga mat and tucks it under her arm then turns toward the door. I follow her down the long entry to the gym and out the door into the main lobby of the hotel. We get on the elevator, and she knows I'm here, but she's acting totally unfazed.

"Are we going to talk about last night?" I ask, leaning up against the wall of the elevator.

"Nope," she says, pushing the button again like it's suddenly going to propel the elevator into turbo speed.

"Maryn," I say, giving her a look. She doesn't respond. I take a step closer to her, letting our arms graze each other. She looks down at them. Finally, we reach her floor, and I escort her off. I follow her down the hall to her room as she digs her keycard out of her gym bag.

She turns to me slowly, looking up at me before she puts it in to open the door. She takes a step closer to me, her eyes studying every inch of my face, and suddenly, I feel really self-conscious.

"In a minute, I'm going to go into that room," she says. "I'm going to take off these leggings, and this tank, and my panties and sports bra. I'm going to get into the shower, let the steaming hot water drip down my body."

I feel my whole body tightening under her breath. *Tell me more, Miss Porter. Or better yet, let me see.*

She steps closer so that her lips are inches from my ears.

"I'm going to run my hands all over my skin, down, down, down," she whispers, and now I feel like my legs are made of rubber. "And while I touch myself, I'm going to imagine you're gone off the face of the planet, never to be heard from again. And *that's* what's going to get me off."

She turns on her heel, opens the door, and slams it in my face. I stand there for a moment in the hallway, dumbfounded, my jaw to the floor. I moan and drop my head to her door. I spin around to walk toward the elevator, and a smile comes over my face.

She knows what she just did to me. She doesn't want to catch the fish, but she sure as hell doesn't want him off the hook yet.

A few hours pass, and I'm finally able to push Maryn out of my mind for a little bit as I study my slides again, reading them off to Rex in the lobby of Landry's headquarters. He's nodding in approval, clapping his big ol' hands, giving me a few pointers. The elevator dings, and off steps Maryn in a perfectly fitted business suit. Her hair is pulled back partially, but not all the way, since I know for a fact she has a hickey behind her left ear.

Rex smiles and waves her over, and she sits down and pulls out her laptop.

"How was your first night in Chicago?" Rex asks her. She clears her throat. Her eyes dart to me for half a second, then she turns and smiles at Rex.

"To be honest, it was a little bit mediocre," she says. "I'm hoping to explore some tonight and do some sight-seeing." He smiles at her and begins giving her restaurant suggestions. She's got her charm all the way turned up, and I can't help but stifle a smile. Mediocre my ass. I have claw marks on my back and remnants of her on my bed that say differently.

Before I know it, the conference room door opens,

and one of the executive assistants escorts us inside. She helps us set up the presentation and gets us some water, and suddenly, I'm feeling unusually nervous. I know we've got the deal, but this is the clincher. This is where I prove to them they haven't wasted their time with us—or millions of dollars. The room starts filling with executives, a bunch of white men who are a bit thick around the middle. They each shake my hand and Rex's, and nod in the direction of Maryn. But after the third or fourth one barely acknowledges her, she takes a step up with us, making herself known. She thrusts her hand out to them and hands a few of them her business card. Rex smiles down at her, proud at her gumption. And it gives me a little bit of confidence that I was feeling slipping away. I take notes from her demeanor and step forward, and then I begin.

I roll through my slides, presenting the rollout of our communications plan with them. I establish all contacts within our company. But as I get to the closing, I feel myself freeze up again. Rex tugs on his jacket in concern, his eyes narrowing on me. I look up sheepishly at Maryn.

Her eyes are wide. And I know she's probably loving this. But this moment is big, a lot more than the weird little game we're playing. She nods at me.

"You got this," she mouths, and suddenly, I'm a brand-new man. I clear my throat and deliver my last few lines. The room is silent for a minute before Don Cable, the CEO of Landry, claps his hands. The rest of the room follows his lead, and I feel the weight of ten elephants evaporate off my shoulders.

"This is beautiful," Don says. "Absolutely perfect. We can't wait to get started with you all."

We all three shake their hands again, make small talk at the little reception they've prepared for us, and then Rex, Maryn and I head out.

It's almost dinnertime by the time we leave, and I'm starving.

"Today was absolutely fabulous," Rex says, waving down the driver he hired to pick us up. "I've got to get back to New York for a few other meetings early tomorrow. But you two should celebrate." He flicks me his company credit card. "On me. Really. Enjoy it."

He drops us at the hotel, and we say our goodbyes. And then Maryn Porter and I are standing awkwardly in our hotel lobby.

"So," I say after a century, "you want to get some grub?"

"I'm starving," she says, "but I don't really need the company. I'm a working girl now. I can foot my own bill."

She turns on her heel, and there goes that goddamn smile on my lips again.

"Maryn," I say, "come out with me."

She turns slowly toward me. It can't be this easy, can it?

Her eyes flick up to mine, and she gives me a slow, warm smile.

"No," she says then gets on the elevator and swiftly closes the doors. I sigh and shake my head as I head back outside to get a cab.

I eat at a local bar that has shitty fries but decent beer prices. Since it's dinner for one, I have my fair share. I take a cab back to the hotel and sleepily get into the elevator. I get to my room and turn the shower on, needing desperately to wash the day off of me. I strip down and pull the shower curtain back just as there's a knock on my door. I freeze and wrap a towel around my waist. I look out the peephole, and I'm dumbstruck. It's her.

"Well, this is unexpected," I say, swinging the door open. Her eyes drop to my abs and slowly trail their way up my chest. She swallows, and I chuckle. "Want to come in?"

She crosses her arms over her chest.

"No," she says. I lean up against the doorway.

"Well, I'm not gonna stand here in my towel," I say. She taps her foot for a moment and bites the inside of her cheek. Then, she throws her hands into the air and grunts before pushing past me and coming inside. I smile and shut the door. "So, to what do I owe the pleasure?" I ask.

She's pacing my room, looking out over the city from the balcony window. Finally, she turns to me.

"I mean it with a whole piece of me when I tell you that I despise you. I've dreamt about fucking you up for years," she says. I nod along, my eyebrows up. I've heard this spiel before. "So, for the life of me, I can't figure out why sex with you is so fucking good."

Okay, that I was not expecting. I drop my arms to my sides and wait for her to go on.

"I shouldn't like it. I should want to continue staying as far away from you as I possibly can," she says. "I was really hoping that when we did it again, it would lose its spark. Or that you'd go soft halfway through or something."

I break out into a laugh, and the faintest smile zips across her lips. I take a few steps toward her. I reach my hand up and tuck a piece of her hair behind her ear. I bend down and lay the most gentle kiss on the nape of her neck. She closes her eyes and drops her head back.

"Care to test your theory?" I whisper, and her eyes open again. She tugs on my towel and lets it fall to the floor. I pull her shirt up over her head and help her shimmy out of her pants, all the while our lips barely leaving each other.

She wraps her arms around my neck and pulls us tighter into each other. But then she pulls away.

"Ahh," she says, stepping back and bringing her hands to her face. "Why is this so hard for me?"

She begins pacing again, and I feel like an idiot standing here in my birthday suit. She pauses and looks me up and down again.

"I mean, it doesn't help that you look like *that*," she says, and I roll my eyes and smile. "But I shouldn't want to keep doing this. Aside from the fact that we now work together, you're literally the one person in the world that my parents despise. You're the one person I shouldn't want to do this with."

I step closer to her, ignoring the comment about her parents. If it came to that, we could get to them later.

"But you want to keep doing it, don't you?" I ask her, the corner of my mouth tugging up into a smile. I lean down and lay a soft, gentle kiss on her lips, letting my tongue trace her bottom lip just once.

She squeezes her eyes shut.

"Sort of," she says. As I'm about to wrap my arms around her, she presses her hands against my chest. "But this has to be completely quiet. No one—and I mean *no one*—can know about this. I can't lose this job. And I can't do this to my parents. Oh, God, my parents," she says, swirling around and sitting down on the couch. The same couch I fucked her on last night.

Suddenly, this feels a bit heavy for me to be naked. I bend down and tie my towel back around my waist.

"I wouldn't do that to you," I tell her, kneeling down in front of her. "I'm not a kiss-and-tell sort of guy." I offer her a smile, and she returns the favor. "Look, this can be as casual as you want."

I need to put the ball in her court. One, because I'm not going to push myself on her. And two, because I don't really think I know what to do with the ball if it *is* in my court right now. I like her body, and I *love* sleeping with her. But I actually like her personality, too. And I'm not sure what to do with that.

"*Extremely* casual," she says. "Just sex. But not like, boring, missionary sex. Sex like we've had. Hot sex."

I can't keep a straight face. I bust out laughing.

"Hot sex," I say. "Deal." She nods and leans back, and I follow her lead. We're silent for a minute, and then she stands up to her feet. She picks up her clothes and starts dressing, and I feel my insides sink. I guess it's weird to have sex the same night you make a deal about having sex.

"Not tonight," she says, making her way to the door. "I need to prove to myself that I can walk away from you at any time, even when you...ugh, even when you look like *that*," she says, holding a hand out to me again. I laugh and nod.

"I understand," I say, following her to the door. "See you in New York."

She turns to me and smiles.

"See ya," she says. I shut the door and sigh, leaning

up against it. I'm about to push off toward the bathroom when there's another knock on my door.

I open it, and she's there again.

"Still want to get that food?" she asks. I smile and wave her inside.

"Yeah, I do," I say. "But I really need to shower first." She nods and sits on the foot of my bed. As I'm walking toward the bathroom, I tug my towel loose and watch as her eyes find me immediately. "You're welcome to join."

13

MARYN

I'm sitting here on the foot of his bed while I hear him moving the shower curtain back. It's up to me; it's my decision. But the window is closing soon. I sigh and begin stripping. Hot shower sex it is.

I tiptoe into the bathroom, hoping to take him a bit by surprise. I move the curtain back, and he turns to me slightly. The sight of his eyes scanning me up and down makes my whole body tingle.

He turns to face me, the beads of water dripping down his brown skin making me melt. His green eyes are bright and sparkling, and I feel myself getting lost in them. I swallow and take a step closer to him as he wraps his arms around me. He leans down to kiss me then pulls me under the water, letting my hair get wet. He spins me around so that my back is to him and begins washing it. Then, his hands slide around to my front, and he grazes my nipples as his fingers trail down. He kisses the side of my neck and tugs on my ear with his teeth, letting his hands slide down to my center. I let out a long moan as he lets his fingers start their work on me, two entering me while his thumb strokes my outside in rhythm. I feel my knees grow weak as I reach my hands out to brace myself against the shower wall. He leans forward and spins me around, pulling me into his warm, wet body.

"I got you, baby," he whispers, "just let go."

It's like my legs are taking orders from him. They spread themselves apart, giving him even more direct access. He works his fingers in and out so quickly that I'm not even sure of what's going on. I drop my head back, letting the water run down my chest. He sucks the droplets off my breasts as he fingers me, my whole body going wild in his arms.

"That's it, Maryn," he groans. "Let it go. Come for me."

And I do. I let out a whimper, my whole body limp. He waits for a beat then sets me down, steadying me. He turns around, finishes washing his own body, and turns the water off. He gets out and hands me a towel, and I'm standing there with my mouth open, completely in awe of him. He smiles as he bends over to kiss my cheek.

"Let's go get that food," he says.

Note to self: take more showers with Wyatt.

I feel a little weird as we get dressed. I didn't even touch him, let alone get him off, and here I am, still shaky and recovering from the near-death experience that was that orgasm.

"Are you...are you sure?" I ask him. He looks at me for a minute, perplexed. He's not sure what I'm asking him, but then he gets it. He smiles, his white teeth bright in the dim room.

"If you think I don't get anything out of doing that

to you, you're wrong." He smiles then pulls a t-shirt on over his head. I say a quick goodbye to his abs as they disappear and then comb my hair out with my fingers and throw it into a braid.

We walk down the street casually as he leads me to a small little Italian place on the corner a few blocks down.

"How do you know about this place?" I ask him as we get seated. It's late now, seeing as we went our separate ways, reconnected in the shower, and still had to walk here. There are only a few people left in the restaurant, so we get seated right away at a little booth in the back of the restaurant.

"I've come here a few times before, whenever I've been out to Chicago," he says.

"Does Caldell have a lot of clients out this way?" I ask, taking a sip of the water in front of me. He shrugs.

"Just a few. One of our contracts is up for renewal this year with a mid-size tech company out here called Bawning. Play your cards right and you might find yourself out here again in a few months—with me," he says with a wink and a smile. I roll my eyes but can't fight my lips from curling up.

"Oh, lucky me," I say, perusing the menu while acting like the thought of being near him isn't totally making my stomach flip.

"Let me ask you a question," he says, leaning back in his seat. "When you picture your life a few years from now, what do you see?"

I give him a look as I lay my menu down.

"Wow, that's deep for two coworkers on a business trip," I say with a nervous laugh. He smiles, but he doesn't laugh. He leans forward a bit in his chair.

"I know this is casual, but based on our track record for hotel rooms, I don't think anything between us is 'just coworkers.'"

My stomach flips again, and I shift in my seat uncomfortably. I know he's right, but I can't admit it.

"Uh, well, I want to have some of my own accounts," I say. "I want to know the ins and outs of the company." I narrow my eyes on his and give him half a smile. "I guess I want *your* job."

He smiles and sits back in his seat, taking a sip of his water.

"Then go after it," he says.

I get pasta, and he gets pizza, and we both pick at each other's plates as we talk, not even noticing we're doing it. It surprises me how easily we can just sit together. Always at the back of my mind, there's that voice—I'm pretty sure it's my father's—telling me to stay away from him. Reminding me of the pain he caused.

But it's hard to hear it over my own laughter when he talks about his first day on the job at Caldell and how he tripped over the stage steps at his graduation from Melladon. But then it happens. He brings up Willa by accident.

"I remember as I was walking over to my parents that day," he says, taking another bite of pizza, "my mom saying something like, 'You're the only kid we have left. Can you please not break your neck?'" He chuckles, but when he realizes the line we've now crossed, he stops.

I wipe my lips with my napkin and set it down on the table, taking a long, drawn-out sip. He clears his throat and looks down at his hands on the table. He pays the bill a short while later with his company credit card, and we walk back to the hotel in complete silence. We get in the elevator; I press 18 and 28.

"Sorry," he mutters just before the doors open. My eyes flick up to him. I swallow.

"You shouldn't be sorry about bringing her up," I say. "I'll see you back in New York."

As I get to my room that night and pack up my things, this overwhelming sadness hits me. Like some-thing got ruined, some spark got drenched before it became a fully lit flame. But that's just the thing. It *can't* be a flame. Because he did have a sister, and now he doesn't. And because of that, in a whirlwind of things that happened that I still can't fully understand, my family almost lost everything. Like a reminder from the freaking heavens, my phone lights up. I smile a sad smile before I hit the answer button.

"Hey, Dad," I say.

14

MARCH 2015 - MARYN

I've been avoiding social media like the plague ever since Dad was put on leave. I can't stand the speculation; I can't stand the chatter. The weird thing is, it's all coming from people who don't really know him. They are spreading horrible rumors; some are even looking him up on the state case search, as if a freakin' traffic ticket could somehow be a sign that someone was a kidnapper—or worse. Some are spreading such outlandish shit it's all I can do not to look up where they live and scream at them. But it won't help. According to Dad's lawyer, it can only hurt us right now. It's best to keep our heads down and stay quiet.

But the chatter. It's so, so loud.

But everything in our house is quiet.

Dad's in front of the television a lot, or in his study. He doesn't have much to do, so he's been doing yardwork a lot now that it's a little bit warmer. It's been two long months since he's been placed on administrative leave with little to no update on when it might come to an end. Luckily, he still gets paid, but teaching is so much more to my dad than a paycheck.

The school board contacts him every few weeks, and our nerves go up on end each time. He gets in his car and drives down to their central office with his lawyer and answers any and all questions as best he can. But the fact is, he doesn't know anything. And they don't, either. They don't have a real reason to keep him on leave, but because there is no answer for Willa's disappearance yet, he's the only solid answer they have to the public's questions.

"It's just your typical case of scapegoating," Dad's lawyer, Eduardo, tells him over the speakerphone while he and Mom are in the study. Tucker and I are spying from the hall. "They have nothing on you, but they have nothing to give to the public. We're going to wait to see if this blows over. If it doesn't, we will file a suit for wrongful termination."

"Termination?" Mom asks. I feel my chest growing tighter.

"There's no way it will get to that point," Eduardo says. "Don't worry. They've got nothing."

We hear Mom and Dad hang up and make their way to the door, so we scramble back to our rooms, pretending like our world isn't going up in flames.

Mom doesn't work. Dad's job is literally our lifeline. But Eduardo says we will be okay. I know he's right. He has to be.

SCHOOL FUCKING SUCKS, if I'm being honest.

My friends still talk to me, but my invites to their outings have become a little more scarce. People who don't know me, and never have, often give me looks or get totally silent as I walk by, as if I'm going to suddenly blurt out that my family and I know Willa's whereabouts or something. My teachers say nothing, which is almost worse than them saying everything. Some of them have been teaching with my dad for twenty years. But suddenly, it's like he disappeared into thin air. They all carry on with their lives like Willa and my dad didn't exist. The letter he got about his leave mentioned in multiple instances that this wasn't for "disciplinary purposes," but that it was more for his own protection during the investigation.

But it sure seems disciplinary. And it sure seems like everyone already thinks he's guilty.

My dad. My sweet, history nerd of a dad who doesn't even raise his voice at his own kids. Like he could be capable of something like this.

Whatever *this* is. There hasn't been an update on Willa in a few weeks. I know they found her headband in the woods not so long ago, but that's the last we've heard. They called Dad down to the police station when they found it, and as always, he cooperated without a word. His lawyer told him he didn't have to; they don't have any evidence to tie him to it except an eyewitness account that he was there and surveillance footage of his car pulling into the parking lot. But Dad keeps reminding us that someone's child is still missing. And he wants to be as helpful as he can be, even if he truly has no clues to offer. After the reports about the headband hit the news, everything lit up again, and we are quickly on the downward slope of the rollercoaster.

"I hope they tested that thing for DNA against that teacher. The brother saw him at the store that night. It's fishy to me," one woman on the news had said before I turned the TV off and chucked the remote across the room. Mom squeezed my hand that night as she walked by.

"It's just a bunch of talk, baby," she had said in a soft, defeated tone.

Sometimes, late at night when everything is quiet, I think about Willa. I wonder what actually happened, how her family sleeps at night, if they even do at all. I think about her brother, too. I saw him during a quick press conference he gave. I saw him when I told him off on his own porch. He graduated before I got to high school, so I didn't know him, but I've grown to hate him. He's the one who placed Dad there. He's the one who said his name and caused all this chaos for us.

But I wonder what it feels like. I think about Tucker. How quiet the house would be, how lifeless everything would feel. I wonder if she's still alive. If whoever has her is taking care of her, or if she's even alive anymore. And it makes me sick.

But there are so many people who are thinking about her right now. And I know it sounds selfish, but we're hurting, too. To watch someone as brave and bold in my life as my father be torn down, it's enough to make anyone drop to their knees. And the worst part is, I can't fix a damn thing for him.

15

WYATT

We've been back in New York for a week now, and I'm disappointed in how few encounters I've had with Maryn. We had a debriefing meeting with Nate and Rex, but it mostly consisted of Rex talking about the presentation and clapping me on the back. She left in a hurry, and that's about the extent of our interaction.

It's so odd, knowing that we were naked together multiple times just days ago, and right now, we're barely acknowledging each other. I literally can't go a moment without thinking about her. The way she laughed at dinner, what she looks like when she's coming undone in my arms, what it feels like when she looks at me. I'm not ready for this—whatever it is—to be done. We need to get over this family hurdle and keep moving.

I'm working late, and most of the sensor lights in the office are slowly starting to click off. Except for one. And it's hers. I stroll out of my office for a casual cup of coffee at six in the evening when I see her typing fever-ishly away at her desk.

"Boss workin' you too hard?" I ask. She doesn't even look up at me; she just smiles for a millisecond and keeps working. "How was your week?"

She finishes typing her thought and then pauses, slowly turning to me.

"Stressful. I have a lot to catch up on from being away last week," she says. Then she turns back to her computer.

"What are you doing tonight?" I ask her. She pauses again and looks around, making sure that we are definitely the only ones here. She sighs. She's wearing glasses today, and the whole sexy librarian thing is fucking hot.

She leans back in her seat and looks up at me.

"Wyatt," she says. I shake my head and smile.

"Don't," I say. Her eyebrows shoot up.

"Don't what?"

"Don't make this a big thing. Our families, all that stuff…it was a long time ago," I say. "This is supposed to be casual, remember?"

She twitches her jaw and crosses her legs, making her pencil skirt pull up a bit.

"But it *is* a big deal, Wyatt," she says. "It doesn't matter how long ago." I scoot closer to her.

"No one knows. And no one will," I say. "Look, I was just gonna go home and order some pizza. I wanted to see if you wanted to join. We don't even have to have hot sex. I'll be here for another twenty minutes or so. Let me know what you decide."

I push off of her desk and walk back into my office. I sit down in my chair and blow out the big breath I was holding in. God, acting like a confident, cocky asshole is a lot of work. Eighteen minutes later, she steps into the doorway of my office with her bag on her shoulder and her arms crossed.

"What sort of deal is this if I don't get hot sex out of it?" she asks.

It takes me by surprise, and I bust out laughing. I shut down my computer and grab my stuff, then meet her at the doorway.

"Let's see where the night takes us," I say, guiding her out and toward the elevators.

We get back to my apartment, and I watch as she looks around and takes it all in. It's no penthouse, but I'm proud of my bachelor pad. I've got a gourmet kitchen with the works, a big master suite, and a pretty decent view of the city. It's served me well in the past with other women who have joined me here. But for some reason, tonight, I don't even care about that. I just missed her. I just want to talk to her.

The pizzas arrive shortly after we do, and I like the way she gets comfortable so quickly. She kicks off her heels and pulls her feet up under her on the couch while I get us drinks.

"So, how is that other big deal coming that Nate was working on?" she asks as she takes a big bite of her pepperoni slice.

"What big deal?" I ask.

"Um," she says, dabbing at her mouth with a napkin, "he said it was some art gallery or something?"

I look at her, perplexed. Did Nate mention something and I totally missed it, or is he getting business without me? Between Maryn and Landry, I've been a little distracted this week, so either are possible. I decide to play the devil's advocate until I talk to Nate. I shrug.

"I've been swamped with some of our other

accounts this week," I say. "He might have mentioned it. I'll touch base with him on it next week."

That answer seems to satisfy her. She finishes a second piece and then wipes her hands and face and leans back on the couch.

"So," she says. "Are we doing this?"

I look at her, my jaw dropping.

"Doing what?"

She gives me a "you know what I mean" look and crosses her arms. She stands up from the couch and takes off her blazer, then slowly starts to unbutton her shirt. I stand up and walk toward her, pressing my hand on top of hers so that they're both on her chest.

"I meant it when I said tonight could just be pizza," I say. Her eyes narrow at me, and she wriggles her hands free to keep unbuttoning.

"And I meant it when I said it wasn't a real deal if I don't get some hot sex out of it," she says. There's something in her eyes that makes me feel guilty, like she feels like she has to sleep with me. I mean, I know I've given her some of my best bedroom work, but I think it's more than that. It's like she's afraid of talking too much. Of getting to know too much. Sex is easier.

But as she's stripping in front of me, her black lacy bra sliding down off of her arms, her nipples pointed straight at me, I realize that I'll take her any way she'll give herself to me.

We start in the living room tonight, and while she's going down on me on the couch, my head is spinning. I return the favor, then bring her to my bedroom. We do doggie style, her on top, and finish with her legs over my shoulders. Every time with her, my body reacts with even more intensity. Like it wasn't ready for her. I'm spooning her, facing the windows in my bedroom.

"Wow," she says, "you have a decent view." I smile and pull the hair back from her neck so I can kiss it.

"You should see it from back here."

She smiles and tilts her head back, melting into my lips. Then, she rolls over onto her stomach so she's facing me.

"Wyatt," she says.

"Yeah?" I say, pulling my hand up to rest my head on it. She pauses for a moment, reaching her hand up to trace my lips, my chin, my jawline. Then, it's like something hits her. Like the freaking clock struck midnight. She shakes her head and slides out of bed. She starts dressing, and I feel my stomach drop.

"You know, you could stay," I say, starting to get sick of this girl leaving me naked and alone. She smiles as she finishes buttoning her shirt and shakes her head.

"Casual," she says, leaning down to plant a long kiss on my lips that feels anything but casual. I close my eyes as she pulls away, not wanting to watch her walk out again. Fuck.

It's the first time in a while that I've wished a weekend away—God knows I need them. But it's Monday, and I will see her today. Watching her leave my apartment did weird things to me.

When I get in, though, she's not at her desk. I casually go through the mail I got at the office as I look around. Nate's office light is out, too.

"Nate out today?" I ask Priscilla.

"He had a meeting," she says. I nod. "He took Maryn with him."

I nod, glad she mentioned it before I had to ask.

I go to my office and shut the door. I pull up Nate's calendar, but it's blocked for a private meeting. It's bugging me that I'm not sure where he is. We share all of our meetings, all our clients, all of the work. I know he's vying for his dad's spot one day, but Rex has alluded to the fact that there could be somewhat of a tug-of-war over it. We don't talk about it much; we keep the friendly competition light. But I'm starting to wonder if the competition is a little less friendly for Nate than it is for me.

I pull out my phone and text him.

Hey, man. Is today the meeting with Space Solutions?

I know it's not. That's next week.

Hey, man. No, this is a potential new client. I don't think it's gonna work out, but I figured it was good to get Maryn's feet wet in the initial process.

I clench my jaw. I'm sort of hating that she's with him, despite the fact that he's her manager.

Ah, gotcha. See you when you get back.

The day seems to take for-fucking-ever, but around lunchtime, Nate and Maryn walk into the office, both carrying carry-out cups. They had lunch together, and it's bugging me more than it should.

I pop my head out of my office just as they're walking by. She pauses awkwardly and tucks a piece of hair behind her ear.

"Hey," I say. "How'd it go?" She looks to Nate.

"Pretty well," he says, "we'll see how it turns out. How were your meetings?"

"All went as planned. So who was this account,

again?" I ask. Nate switches from one foot to the other awkwardly. His blond hair is curly and usually tame, but today, it looks a little more unruly to me. He's really just Rex, thirty years younger. He clears his throat.

"This small art gallery in Midtown. I think we're way out of budget for them, but they wanted us to come down." He says it with a casual shrug.

I'm about to ask the name when he turns to Maryn.

"So you'll work on that communications plan for them?" he asks. She nods.

"Of course," she says. He smiles and nods.

"Thanks for coming along today. You did great," he says. She smiles and waves as she walks back to her desk. I clench my jaw again as they both disperse back to their desks.

I walk back to my own and start searching for art galleries in Midtown Manhattan, but there are quite a few, and none appear to be new. I reach for my desk phone and dial Maryn's extension.

"Hello?" she answers.

"Hey," I say, "do you mind popping in my office for a minute?"

She pauses on the other end of the phone.

"Uh, sure," she says. I hear her heels click across the office as she makes her way to my doorway. She pauses there.

"Come on in," I say. She comes in but not before taking a look behind her to make sure no one notices.

She takes a seat and smooths out her dress pants.

"What was the name of the gallery you guys went to today?" I ask her. She swallows and looks back out the door, like she's still looking for someone.

"It doesn't have a name yet," she says. I raise an eyebrow.

"Huh?"

"They are just getting started," she says. "The owner is someone Nate knew from high school or something."

I nod slowly.

"Did he ask you not to talk about it?" I ask her straight out. She swallows again then stands.

"Not in so many words," she says, "but he doesn't want to talk about it much until he knows if it's going to pan out. And he's my manager. So if he wanted to keep it quiet, I would have. Especially from you."

I lean back in my chair and fold my hands on my lap.

"Oh? And why is that?"

"I told you," she says, heading for my door. "I'm here in *spite* of you." She pauses for a moment, then her lips curl into a devilish smile, and I can't keep from doing the same.

As good as she looks walking away, though, my mind travels back to this gallery. I need to know what sort of unnamed art gallery that's popping up in New York City would be looking for a PR agency before it even has a name or a website.

I'm about to walk into Nate's office, though, when my cell phone rings on my desk.

"Hey, Ma," I say. "How are you?"

I pause when I hear her crying on the other end of the line.

16

MARYN

I'm typing away at my desk, already halfway through the proposal that Nate asked me to put together for this gallery. I'm really excited about this project because it's the first one that Nate is really letting me take by the reins. He's letting me act as the account manager if we get the deal, and I'm already picturing my email signature with a new title after I get a huge promotion. Okay, maybe I'm getting a little bit ahead of myself. But like Nate said, there's not a huge risk, because they don't have a ton of brand equity yet.

I like Nate. He's definitely got the whole salesman, pushy-but-no-too-pushy thing down pat—a character-istic I know he got from his dad. He says all the right things, makes easy conversation, and I have yet to be in a meeting with him where he doesn't make the client smile. I'm learning a lot from him.

But the guy in the office down the hall from him...I get the feeling I'm not the only one who has some friendly fire going on with him. It wasn't *what* Nate said about Wyatt; it was *how* he said it. There was a sort of smugness in his tone when I brought up Wyatt and the gallery deal. Nate smiled and shook his head and said, "The details of this will stay between us right now. Wyatt has some bigger fish to fry."

I didn't press it, but it did surprise me. Till now, the two of them seemed thick as thieves and seemed like they worked together perfectly. But I got the feeling on that car ride back to the office that things might not be as smooth-sailing as I had originally thought.

Ha. That makes two of us.

I wanted to stay in that apartment with him all damn weekend. And he freakin' asked me to. But every time I feel myself slipping with him, I picture my dad's face that first time Brady showed up on our doorstep to take him down to the precinct. The big red letters that spelled out "LATE" on the mortgage statements I found in his study. The headlines in the local papers.

Sex, well, that's different. I've already crossed that line. I'm looking at it as more of an exercise, a recreational activity to blow off some steam.

Nevermind the fact that every time I'm with him, I want to stay longer. I want to learn more. I want to talk to him and watch his green eyes light up when he talks about work or the Yankees.

About his sister.

I don't know why the most attractive human I've ever touched, why the best sex I've ever had, just has to be the one man who changed the course of my family's lives forever.

What kind of shit luck is that?

Maryn luck—that's what that is.

I finish the first draft of my proposal, read through it again, then send it off to Nate for his input. Most of the people around me have already left for the day, but I'm not one to run off at five. In fact, I think I am much more productive when there are less people around me. Well, except for the tall, mocha, and handsome executive who always seems to stay late, too. We've enjoyed one too many flirty elevator rides alone together, and very few of them haven't ended in us getting into bed together.

I haven't brought him back to my apartment for the simple fact that Ellie doesn't know. I actually think I could tell her; it's not like her track record is squeaky clean. But I don't want to. There's something about our...whatever it is...staying between us that makes it more exciting. Exhilarating. Even sexier, if that's at all possible.

I look up to see if he's in his office, and to my delight, his light is still on. But as I'm finishing packing up my things, he's moving quickly to shut off the lights and slam the door behind him, not once looking back to my desk to see if I'm still here. It sort of pisses me off. I close my things up and hurry after him, trying to make it look casual but also wanting to be close to him and not miss a chance for another possible elevator escapade.

I'm literally running in my pumps to catch the elevator, but he never turns back. I throw my hand through the doors to stop them from closing, then get on, breathless.

"Couldn't have checked to see if someone needed a lift?" I ask him, blowing a piece of hair out of my face.

I expect a chuckle, or a smile, or even an apology since he's normally such a gentleman. But I get none of the above. There's a scowl on his face, his eyebrows knit together with such intensity that it knocks the wind out of me. He scratches the back of his neck and nods.

"Sorry," he says. I lean back against the wall and press the lobby button, which it looks like he forgot to do.

"You okay?" I ask him.

He doesn't say anything, just shakes his head.

I feel a twinge of guilt. Could this have to do with the gallery and all the secrets?

"Everything alright?" I ask again. He drops his head back against the wall.

"I said I'm fine," he says. His voice has this dark tone to it that I'm not used to, and I don't like it in the least.

"What's going on?" I ask. "Is this about Nate?"

His emerald eyes flick up to me, and he narrows them.

"No. It's not about Nate," he says.

"Are you sure? Because you've been acting weird ever since I told you about it," I say, crossing my arms over my chest. He sighs and rubs his eyelids.

"It's not about that."

"Look, I'm not going to go against my manager's wishes. You might be trying to sabotage me, but—"

"Maryn, it has nothing to do with that," he says again. Yeah, right. I know what a man with his panties in a bunch looks like. And one's standing right in front of me.

"Are you threatened by him?" I ask. His eyes flick up to me again, narrowing even more.

He steps closer to me, then closer, almost so that I'm standing with my back flush to the elevator wall.

"Not in a million fucking years," he growls just

above a whisper. "Enjoy being the gopher for the second-best executive here." There's a ding, and the elevator doors open.

He stalks out, and I storm after him.

"What the fuck is your deal?" I ask him, my voice loud. There's no one around, but even if there was, I don't think I'd be keeping myself much quieter. He just shakes his head and keeps walking, and I feel this burning in my chest with each step he takes. "God, this was such a mistake."

He pauses when I say that and half turns to me, his hand on the door.

"What?"

"Me. You. Me taking this stupid job, letting you into my pants over and over again. Should've followed my gut. You're the same asshole you've always been," I say. "Just looking out for yourself without a care in the world about who you could be hurting in the process." He turns a little more but never looks at me.

"He's up for fucking parole, Maryn," he says. My spine goes straight, and I have to remind myself to breathe.

"Wha...what?" I ask, taking a step closer. Oh, God. I'm such an idiot.

"The guy...the *actual* guy who killed her. He's up for fucking parole," he says. He turns to me all the way, his eyes glazed over with an ice-cold stare. "So, like I said, nothing to do with you or fucking Nate. And yeah, maybe it was a mistake, you taking this job. Because I sure as hell know it was a mistake choosing you."

He turns back and pushes the door open, the wind blowing his suit jacket as he steps into the street.

I stand there, hands at my sides, my bag sliding off my shoulders.

I couldn't keep my fucking mouth shut.

Jesus Christ, Maryn. It's not all about you.

I watch as he disappears into the Manhattan crowd, and the lump in my throat is thick and fiery.

After all these years, all this time, all the hatred I felt toward him, and even after we started hooking up, I have never once apologized for the death of his sister. Not that it had anything to do with me, or my family, but I have barely even acknowledged it.

I've been so busy thinking that he owed me—which, in some ways, is still true—that I never stopped to really grasp the fact that his sixteen-year-old sister was snatched right from under his nose and never returned. He was the last one to see her and, no doubt, feels her loss the heaviest.

Just as the tears start to prick my eyes, my phone buzzes in my hand.

"Hello?" I answer.

"Hey," Ellie says. "You coming home tonight?"

I contemplate her answer for a few moments. She knows I've been hooking up with someone, but I showed her a picture of some other guy at work to throw her off the scent of Wyatt. But I need to let her sniff out the truth.

"Yeah," I say.

"You okay?"

"Not really." She pauses for a moment.

"Okay. Come home," she says. God, I love Ellie.

I barely acknowledge another human on the train ride home, going through the familiar motions without savoring any of the sights or sounds of the city I've grown to love so much. When I walk through our apartment door, I drop my stuff off on the coffee table and collapse onto our oversized loveseat that Ellie's parents got us from Pottery Barn.

She comes out in tiny pajama shorts and a tank top, her hair in a bun. She got a job at a high-end restaurant a few weeks ago, saying she's not sure yet if she wants to pursue a career in philosophy anymore. But at least she's working, and honestly, with the tips she's getting, she's probably better off doing what she's doing.

She leans over the kitchen bar and grabs a plate of chicken and mashed potatoes that she has all ready for me. She hands it to me then grabs a glass of wine she's already poured. Like I said, I love her.

I look down at the food, but I'm not feeling particularly hungry. The wine, though, I can handle.

I sigh and look at her.

"Wait, before you start," she says, pulling out her phone, "Keely wants to check in." I hear the ringing of the video call, then Keely's face pops up.

"What's up, bitch?" she asks. I smirk at her familiar vulgarity. "Why the long face?"

I sigh and rub my temples.

"So, that guy I've been hooking up with…" I say, watching as their eyebrows raise collectively at the same time. "It's actually Wyatt."

"Fucking told you, Ellie!" Keely shouts.

"Dammit! I owe you five bucks," Ellie says.

"What?" I ask.

"Oh, come on," Keely says, and I can hear her snarl through the phone. "You really think we couldn't figure it out? All secretive, staying out late, virtually no details on the actual sex itself? It had to be him you were hiding."

"Yeah, plus that Ricky guy you showed us was def not your type," Ellie says. I roll my eyes and let out a chuckle of surrender. Of course they knew.

"So, what's going on with the big, bad, boss-man?" Keely asks.

"I was kind of an ass today," I say. "I mean, I don't owe him anything. We have an arrangement, and nothing more can come of it because he is who he is and I am who I am. There's too much baggage there."

"But…" Ellie says, egging me on with her hand.

"He was acting all weird after work today, and I thought he was being an ass because I've been working on this sort of secret project with my boss."

"Why is the project a secret?" Keely asks. I shrug.

"I don't know. I have a feeling there's some competition between the two of them," I say with a shrug. "But anyway, I called him out on it. Told him he was the same ass I always thought he was."

"Whoa," Ellie says.

"Yeah. But it turns out, he found out that the guy who killed his sister—the *actual* guy—is up for parole."

Keely whistles. Ellie's eyes grow wide.

"Damn," Keely finally says. "That's fucked up. How can you get parole after murdering a kid?"

I lean back in my seat. I don't know. I don't know any of the details because I didn't ask, and he wouldn't have stuck around long enough for me to, anyway.

"I'm not sure. I don't know much. I just know that I was a bitch about it," I say.

"Well," Keely says, "this could go one of two ways."

I settle back into the chair, knowing I'm in for a Keely lesson.

"First, you can just let it go. Like you said, you don't owe him anything. You had no way of knowing what it was about, and yeah, it was a little self-centered of you to think it was about you and your boss, but whatever. He's still the dude that fucked you over all those years ago."

I nod. Option one is, basically, the mantra I'd been repeating to myself in my head on the way home.

"And option two?" Ellie asks.

"Option two, you could apologize. Talk to him about it. Be nice about it. *But*…beware that might mean you're crossing that whole hook-up-only line," Keely warns. I swallow. Because this is what I wanted to do the second he stormed out of that building.

I nod slowly.

"I want to do that," I say quietly. They both stare back. "I can't imagine what that feels like."

"Then do it," Keely says matter-of-factly.

"But...that line…"

"Might just have to be erased," Keely says with a shrug. Ellie nods in agreement. "Plus, no one has to know. You can be there for him and not a soul—especially your parents—has to know."

I nod and take a swift bite of my potatoes. Suddenly, I have a little more of an appetite. I tell Keely I love her, finish off my plate, and change into something more comfortable. I'm in yogas and an oversized hoodie when I head to the front door.

"Go. Be a *friend,*" Ellie says with a wink. I roll my eyes.

"I'll be back later," I tell her.

I grab a cab and head uptown to his apartment building, my heart thumping in my chest. I hop out and walk into the lobby, when my phone vibrates in my hand.

I can't hear anything but the blood rushing through my ears.

"Hey, Dad," I say, my voice low.

"Hey, kid," he says. "What are you up to?"

"Oh," I say, swallowing and looking around like he can see me from Tilden. "Just about to have dinner with a coworker. Everything okay?"

"Yeah, yeah. All's good. Just saw on the news that the man who killed Willa Mills is up for parole," he says. I swallow. Before I can say anything, he goes on. "They mentioned her brother. Did you know he also works at Caldell?"

My heart is throbbing in my chest. I walk across the lobby and lean up against one of the walls.

"Uh, yeah, someone had told me that," I say. I hear my mother in the background.

"Did you know that before you took the job?" she asks, her voice shrieky and slightly more accusatory than my dad's.

"No, of course not," I lie. "But we don't work together or anything, so it's not like I have to be in contact with him."

I swallow. I have never blatantly lied to my parents, and I am not a fan of the after-feeling.

"Oh, good," Mom says, closer to the receiver now. "If you do, you should request some sort of boundary between you through HR. Some sort of conflict of interest, something or other."

I nervously laugh.

"I'm not sure that exists, Ma," I say. "Unfortunately, he hasn't done anything to me—directly," I add quickly, "that could justify something like that. But I'll definitely keep my guard up. I can handle him."

"That's my girl," Dad says. Mom shouts that she loves me as she's walking away from the phone. I hear my dad take a deep breath.

"Did you know her brother started a support group for family members of missing people?" Dad asks me. "It's actually some sort of foundation."

"I had heard that somewhere," I say, thinking about the fact that all this time with Wyatt, it's never once come up. There's a long pause, then I hear Dad sigh on the other end.

"I hope that man doesn't get parole," he says quietly, and my heart shatters. My dad, still the same gentle soul he's always been.

"Yeah, me either," I say. "Well, I'm gonna head to dinner, Dad. I'll call you guys later. Love you."

I hit end and throw my head back against the wall. I stare at the elevators ahead of me. I so badly want to get in and press the 20 button. But I can't. Not now. I'm not the most spiritual person, but that call, at this time, in this place—that's gotta be a sign. It's a sign I should leave and get back to hating him, and now, most likely, letting him hate me.

I sigh and hang my head as I walk back toward the big glass doors.

"Maryn?" I hear him ask. "What are you doing here?"

17

APRIL 2015 - WYATT

I've been back at school for a little while now, and it feels fake. I was able to keep up with all my classes from Tilden, but there are a few big projects I need to be in Florida for to finish up the semester before graduation.

My parents pushed me to go; they said there was no use in all three of us walking around like zombies. And they're right.

I'm on track to graduate with an almost-perfect GPA —damn that stupid chemistry class my sophomore year —and honestly, it's good to be back at Melladon. I've missed my friends; I've missed the beach; I've missed things that didn't fully revolve around my missing sister.

But every time I take a drink, or smile, or make a joke, I hear Willa's voice in the background. I feel her presence, and I'm hit with a heavy reminder that she's gone. No one knows where or why. She might need me. She could be calling out for me, begging for me to find her. To save her.

And I can't. Because no one on fucking Earth knows where she is.

As I'm walking across campus to my car, my phone rings, and my stomach drops, just as it does whenever my parents call.

"Hey, Ma," I say, nodding to a few people as I walk.

"Hi, hon," she says, her voice still low and sad.

"What's going on?" I ask. I can't tell you the last time one of my parents has called just to check in.

"Well, we got a call from the detectives today," she says. "They are going to go ahead and clear Joe Porter as a suspect."

I swallow.

"What? How?" I ask.

She clears her throat, and I can tell how badly she's trying not to cry. I picture her eyes, big and green, filled with tears.

"Ma?"

"There was another surveillance camera on the backside of the shopping center. It hadn't been at the right angle, but after reviewing it again, they were able to see him getting into his car with his groceries. Alone."

I try to swallow as I slam my car door shut and throw my bag into the back.

"So? What if he went back in? I saw a dark SUV pull away, Ma. I saw it," I say, my own voice cracking. We can't give up. This Porter guy is the only fucking lead we have. The only shot at finding her.

"Well, there's something else," Mom says. "He got into his car at 9:09 p.m. That's fourteen minutes after you saw the car pull out."

"Well, I could have had the time wrong. I mean, I was all stressed, and—"

"The same camera also caught another SUV leaving, baby. It even picked up a partial plate. And it was right at the same time you remembered seeing the car leave."

I don't know what to say, think, or feel. I throw my head back against my headrest.

"So, do we have another lead?" I ask, my heart throbbing with hopelessness and hope all at the same time.

"We might, baby. We might. They are checking the DMV records now to see if we can get any matches."

I close my eyes and nod.

So, the teacher's out. But someone else is in.

18

WYATT

I'm walking into my apartment building with a bag of Chinese food when I see her walking toward me. I do a double-take, because after the things we said to each other earlier, I didn't imagine we'd be seeing each other again. At least, not for a while. And to be honest, I haven't thought about it much. This whole parole thing is weighing heavy on me.

"Maryn?" I ask her as her pretty blue eyes flash up to me. "What are you doing here?"

She stares back at me, her eyes wide and her lips parted slightly. She's clutching her bag to her body, and I can see a bottle of wine sticking out of it. I look back up to her.

"I...uh," she says, sheepishly tucking a piece of her golden hair behind her ear. It's funny, but as pissed as I was today—as pissed as we *both* were—seeing her again makes everything feel just a little bit lighter. She sighs and raises her eyes to me. "I thought you might want to talk. And if not," she says, pulling the bottle out of the bag slightly, "I thought you might want to get wasted and forget about everything."

I lean back on my foot for a minute, looking her up and down. This doesn't feel like the arrangement we discussed, and yet, now that I know that just being with her is on the table, I can't think of anything I want more.

I can't help but give her a half-smile and nod toward the elevators.

"Come on up," I say. She smiles as we walk in together. I can't keep from checking her out the whole elevator ride up. Yoga pants really are God's gift to Earth, and the way they hug her curves is making it hard for me to think about anything else. She's wearing an oversized Tilden High sweatshirt, and she's like the perfect damn concoction of adorable and dangerously sexy. The elevator dings, and I let her off first. I like that she knows how to get to my apartment. It makes it feel like this—whatever it is—is a little more real.

She waits for me to let her in then slips her shoes off —another thing I like. She pulls the bottle from her bag and goes into the cupboard where she knows I keep the wine glasses. She opens the drawer to the right of the sink where she knows I keep the corkscrew, and I realize just how much she really does know. I like her being here. I like her being comfortable. It's hot.

I set the food down and take out two plates, but she holds her hands up.

"I just ate, I'm good," she says. I give her a look and hold up the container.

"It's Sesame Chicken, extra spice," I say. Her eyebrow shoots up.

"Okay, fine," she says, and I chuckle. This isn't the

first time we've indulged in carry-out together. Although, the other times, we've been a lot less clothed.

She pulls out one of the barstools and looks up at me as I'm preparing our plates.

"So," she says, sipping her wine, and I'm preparing for the typical questions I had gotten for so long after Willa went missing.

How are you doing? How's your family? Do you still miss her? You're in our thoughts. I can't even imagine.

But instead, she takes a different route.

"My parents found out today that you work at Caldell," she says. I flick my eyes up to her as I spoon extra sauce over our plates.

"Oh?"

"Yeah, apparently, they mentioned you on the news today when they mentioned the...uh, guy," she says.

"How did that go?"

"They wanted to make sure I didn't have to see you," she says, looking down into her glass as she swirls it around. "My mom wanted me to file a grievance or something, saying I needed to be kept away from you."

I swallow nervously. But to my surprise, she actually starts to laugh. "I told them it wasn't possible seeing as how you've never done anything to me directly."

Then, she gives me this hot-as-hell, mischievous smile. "They don't need to know about what you've done to me in Florida. Or Chicago. Or here in Manhattan."

I smile and shake my head, handing her the plate and taking a seat next to her.

"Well, that's...a lot," I say, scratching my head before I take a bite. "So, what are you going to do about it?"

She looks up at me, spinning her stool around so that she's completely facing me.

"Not a damn thing," she says, her voice dropping just above a whisper. I smile again and knock my knee against hers lightly.

"How come you've never mentioned your foundation?" she asks me. I look down to my plate, finishing my last bite. I clear my throat.

"I don't know. I mean, it's not something that comes up in daily conversation." I shrug. She nods. "There's only a handful of people that totally understand what I...what my family and I...went through. So I guess I just leave it all there with them in the meetings." She nods again.

"How often do you have them?" she asks.

"We try to get together at least every other month. It's tough because, like I said, it's a small group. Some of them come from pretty far away to meet," I say. I can tell she wants to ask more. I look up at her. "I have one in a few weeks, actually. If you want to, you could come?"

She looks up to me, and a flicker of a smile crosses her lips.

"I'd like that," she says.

We finish eating, making comfortable small talk about a few things at work (she conveniently leaves the gallery job out of the conversation) then clean up and walk over to the couch. She makes herself comfortable again, shimmying a little bit closer, closing the gap between us.

"So," she says again, "how does someone who kidnapped and killed a sixteen-year-old get the possibility of parole?"

Her question hits me like a ton of bricks, but I've learned that when Maryn comes in, she comes in hot and heavy. There are no brakes with her; she's more to the point than a damn needle.

I lean my head back against the couch, slouching into the cushions. She scoots a little closer to me, resting her head on her fist as she looks at me.

"I have no fucking idea," I say, swiping a hand over my face. "This justice system is so fucked up."

She nods in agreement.

"When is his hearing?" she asks.

"Two weeks. And I'm…" I feel my voice crack, and my hand starts to shake. I put my glass down on the coffee table and lean forward, dropping my head in my hands. I'm not strong enough to go through all of this again. It's bullshit. She scoots even closer, and I feel the warmth of her hand press against my back, her other hand dropping to my leg.

"This is fucking bullshit," she whispers. I nod and take a deep breath.

"He was caught. His DNA confirmed it. How is it even possible?" I ask. Her hand starts to rub my back now, and I can't get over how good it feels, how it makes me feel instantly calmer. My problems won't be solved from her sitting with me, but somehow, now, it feels like I can take them on.

"I'm sorry, Wyatt," she says. "You shouldn't have to go through this again." Her hand is rubbing my thigh now, and she scoots forward a bit more and takes one of mine into hers. She squeezes it then lets go. But I squeeze back and hold onto it. I turn to her slowly.

"Wyatt," she says, her eyes at the ground. "I need to say something to you." I swallow.

"Okay."

"I'm sorry about your sister," she says. I swallow again, but it's harder this time. I blink a few times then look at her.

"What do you mean? Why are you sorry?" I ask.

"I'm just...I'm sorry about what happened to her. I've been angry for a long time. I was really angry then, and it never really went away. And what happened to us...it was bad, but we still had each other. You didn't," she says, and I feel this burning in my chest. "So, I'm sorry. I really am. Willa was a sweet girl, and nobody deserves what happened to her."

I squeeze her hand and draw in another breath.

"Well, I'm sorry, too," I say. Because I am. "When I remembered that I had seen your dad that night at the store, it felt like maybe I was going to be the one to figure it out. Maybe I wasn't too late to save her; maybe I was going to be able to stop my parents from being in so much pain. So I said your dad's name. I thought if we could point them in the right direction, everything would happen faster. I never once stopped to think about the implications it would have on your dad if it wasn't true, or if it turned out he wasn't involved. Or your family. Or you." Suddenly, I feel something I haven't felt in years, and that's an overwhelming urge to cry.

I haven't shed a lot of tears since my sister died. It takes a lot out of you to go through that, so your body tends to put up some protective walls to stop it from happening again.

I draw another slow breath and look into her eyes again, and to my surprise, there are tears in hers, and it's tearing up whatever's left inside of my chest.

"Wyatt," she whispers again.

"Yes?"

"I don't hate you," she mutters. Her eyes find mine again slowly. I reach my hand out and let my thumb stroke her chin then her bottom lip. My other hand cups her cheek, and I pull her lips to mine. She pulls herself up onto her knees as she wraps her arms around my neck. Her tongue dives into my mouth, and it takes me back. I pull my head away.

"Tell me again," I whisper. Her eyes are searching my face.

"I don't hate you," she says again, and I pull her back into me. "I don't hate you at all."

My hands are running up and down her back, and she's cupping my face as we kiss. Every time our lips touch, it's like I become more and more dependent on them. Like I won't be able to breathe, eventually, without them. She pushes up against me then holds her arms up so I can slide the hoodie off over her head. Her t-shirt comes with it, and to my surprise, she's not wearing anything underneath it. I hold my arms up and let her do the same, and I love watching the way she takes me all in. She presses against me, and I wrap my arms around her as we fall back against the couch. Lying here with her, skin to skin, makes me breathless without even doing anything.

Her fingers trail up my body, then one hand slips down into my waistband, and I let out a gasp when she grabs hold of me. She lets out a small moan of delight when she realizes that I'm already ready for her and lets her hand work on me as our lips move together.

I let her go for a few moments, breaking our kisses to drop my head back as it explodes with pleasure. She grabs my head and kisses my neck, my shoulder, my chest. I slip her hand out of my pants and shimmy to the edge of the couch, pulling down my sweats and my boxers. I scoot over to her and help her get rid of the yogas, then I pull her into me again. I kiss her lips, her jawline, her ear, her neck. I wrap my hand around her head and lay her back against the couch and lower myself onto her. I'm staring down at her, and I've never seen anything, or anyone, so fucking beautiful. Her locks are all out of her bun now, floating around the cushion. She reaches up and pulls me down to her, kissing me gently then biting my bottom lip before letting me go.

"Wyatt," she says just as I'm getting myself into position. I look down at her. "I want you. And not just like this."

I feel like I've crashed into a wall. My arms feel weak as I hold myself over her. Because goddamn if I don't want her, too. I lower my lips down to her face, kissing it again. I bring them to her ear

"You have me, then," I tell her just as I push myself inside of her. I groan as we begin to move, and she wraps her legs around me, holding me tight to her body, pushing me deeper and deeper inside of her. We move back and forth together, kissing in sync with our rhythm, moving like we're fucking pros with each other's bodies. I feel her nails dig into my back as she clenches around me, and not even a moment later, I'm spent, too. I fall on top of her, both of us catching our breath. It takes a moment for her to release her legs, like she doesn't want me to move as badly as I don't want to.

As I finally pull myself up, I lower down for one more long kiss.

This was different.

We've done way more, touched way more, explored way more of each other the other times we've hooked up.

But this *felt* like *way* more. I get up and grab her some paper towels before joining her back on the couch. When she's done, she comes back and snuggles up against me, and I wrap the throw that hangs off the back of the couch around us. Her head is against my chest, and I'm pretty sure there's not one part of me that's not touching a part of her.

My heart rate has finally slowed, and the realization of why she's here in the first place is slowly creeping back in. I feel my grip on her tighten, like I'm afraid that if she goes, I'll wake up in that goddamn parole meeting.

"Maryn," I whisper.

"Hmm?" she moans against my chest.

"Please don't leave tonight," I say without opening my eyes. I don't want to see her reject me. But to my surprise, I feel her lips press up against my skin.

"Wasn't planning on it," she says. I smile and run my fingers through her hair. There she goes again, making me feel like I can do anything.

19

MARYN

I wake up with this weird kink in my neck, and after I peel my eyes open, I realize it's because we're still on the couch. I feel his warm body pressed up against mine, our hands still clasped, and I smile.

I should have started staying over a while ago.

I don't want to move, because I don't want this to be over, but I also can't feel my right arm. I shift slightly, but it's just enough to wake him.

He opens his eyes and blinks a few times then gently readjusts his arm under me. I turn to face him, letting my palm land on his cheek and my thumb trace his bottom lip.

"You're still here," he says with that killer grin. If I were wearing underwear, they'd probably have dropped to the ground with that.

"Of course," I say, pushing myself up and kissing his lips.

"Thank you," he whispers before kissing me again, and it makes my chest tighten. He needed me last night, and it feels good. "Want some breakfast?"

I smile and nod, and he scooches out from underneath me but not before I spank his perfect ass and whistle. He rolls his eyes as he pulls his pants on. He reaches down for his shirt, but I stop him.

"I'd rather you didn't," I say. "I prefer my breakfast with a view."

He laughs and throws his head back then does as he's told and drops his shirt back to the floor. I freshen up in the bathroom as he starts making some sort of fancy omelet. When I come back into the kitchen, it smells like a five-star restaurant. He serves my food within a few minutes, and I'm attacking it like I haven't eaten in years.

"Jesus, this is good," I say between bites. He smiles as he leans across the bar, eating his own.

"Glad you like it," he says. "So," he goes on, a mischievous look in his eye, "you don't hate me, huh?"

I put my fork down and smile, rolling my eyes playfully.

"Oh, Lord, are you gonna throw that in my face?" I say, crossing my arms over my chest.

"Hey, you said it, not me," he says with a shrug. He gathers our plates and puts them in the sink then comes around to the other side of the bar.

He gently pushes my legs apart and stands between them, putting a hand on the bar on either side of me. He leans down and kisses me, and it's a long, slow, leaves-me-panting sort of kiss.

"So if you don't hate me, what does that mean?" he asks, resting his forehead on mine for a moment before rolling off and leaning down to kiss my neck. I moan and drop my head back so he can continue.

"It means that I want to be around you," I say. He kisses back up my neck.

"Uh-huh," he says, then he kisses my jawline.

"And it means that our hot sex is about to get way hotter," I say, and he laughs, kissing down my cheek to my lips.

"Go on," he whispers, kissing up the other side of my face.

"And it means that I don't want anyone else kissing you or having hot sex with you."

He pauses at my ear, and I swallow. I can't believe I just said that out loud. I hate coming across as needy, especially with a guy. But it's true. I don't want him going down on any other girl with that god-sent tongue or making her to-die-for omelets. He pulls his face back from mine and looks down at me.

"Do you think I've been seeing someone else?" he asks. I shrug.

"I hadn't really thought about it. It wasn't really my business," I say. "But I guess I sort of want it to be my business now."

He takes my chin in his fingers and tilts my head back. He leans down and kisses me, long and slow again, but this time letting his tongue massage mine. He pulls back, nibbling on my bottom lip before stepping back.

"I haven't been with anyone else since Florida," he says. "And I don't intend to."

I smile and nod. He pulls me up off the barstool so he can kiss me again, running his hands down my back and resting them on my ass. "But that goes for you, too."

I nod and give him a fake salute.

"And no more lunch dates with Nate," he says,

nuzzling my neck. I push him back gently and shoot him a look.

"He's my boss. I'll get lunch with him if he wants," I say. He can tell work is a boundary I won't cross. "Speaking of that, I won't compromise my job or how hard I've been working," I tell him. "Not even for you. So don't ask me to. Don't ask me about the gallery; don't ask me questions you know I can't answer."

He's looking at me, eyes narrowed, but he's got a smile on his face.

"You're too good of a worker," he says with a smile. "But fine, deal. Just be careful with Nate. I don't know what he's up to." I roll my eyes.

"I can handle myself, Mr. Executive, but thank you," I say, pushing myself up against him and biting his neck gently.

"Speaking of work," he says, "what do we do about it?"

"What do you mean?"

"I mean, we're together, right?" he asks, and it makes me smile. It's like we're having "the talk" in high school.

"Yes, Wyatt," I say, "we're together. But it doesn't need to go on public broadcast. Like I said, this can't screw up my job for me. I need it."

He nods and takes my hand, looking down at our clasped fingers. I step closer to him. "But when we're alone in the elevator, feel free to whisper dirty things to me."

His eyes light up as I kiss him and walk away, leaning down to grab my hoodie.

"Heading out?" he asks, and I can't help but notice the disappointment in his voice. I freeze. I don't really have anything to do today. Ellie is working the lunch shift, and it's a rainy Saturday in Manhattan. I turn back to him slowly.

"I just thought you might be sick of me," I say with a smile. He saunters over to me, taking the hoodie gently from my hands and dropping it on the couch.

"Never," he says.

After a spicier round two of last night that lands me on my back on his cool kitchen counter before an a-*may*-zing finale on his kitchen table, we're watching reruns of *Martin* while snacking on chips and guac.

"I don't think I'm ever gonna get sick of your penis," I blurt, thinking out loud about how perfect every inch of him is. It makes him choke on his chip for a minute before he turns to me, laughing hysterically.

"*What?*" he asks, exasperated. I chuckle and shrug.

"I'm serious. It's like sex with you gets better every single time we have it," I say. He smiles and leans in to me. He kisses my cheek then slides down to my lips.

"I don't think I'm ever gonna get sick of *any* part of you," he says. His fingers trail down my stomach and rest just on top of my hottest spot over my yogas. "But yes, I don't think I'll ever get sick of *her* either."

I smile and kiss him back.

"On that note, before I jump you again, what do you say to lunch?" he asks, hopping up from the couch. He holds a hand out to me, and I take it.

This is the first time we will be out together in New York since we've decided to be *together*-together.

"Let's do it," I say. But then I look down at myself. "But do you mind if we stop at my apartment so I can change? The walk-of-shame thing is one thing, but the lunch-of-shame thing is a different level."

"Sure," he says with a smile. "Lead the way."

This is the first time he's going to be in my apartment, and I suddenly feel a little self-conscious. Our apartment is usually pretty clean, but I would put the hot-guy-coming-over spin on it if I had some time to prepare. I pull my phone out and text Ellie in case she hasn't left yet. She's a fan of walking around in her underwear, which wouldn't be the best first impression.

Oh, dammit! I'm already on my way to work. Bring him back so I can meet him!

I smile at my phone.

"Ellie won't be there, but she says you have to come back so she can meet you," I tell him as we get in the cab. He smiles.

"I'm down," he says. "I want to meet whoever you want me to meet."

Then our eyes flick up to each other, and I know we've had the same thought: my parents. If this turns into something, how in the *fuck* would I tell my parents? I can almost picture how that would go.

Never mind, I don't want to.

He takes my hand and squeezes it.

"It's all gonna be fine," he tells me, and I'm awestruck at how he can read my mind. "We'll figure it out." He slips his arm around my shoulders and tucks me into him as he looks out the window. And as I let his warmth surround me, I know he's right. We pull up to my building, and I let the cabbie know we're here. It's not as glamorous as his end of town, but I'm proud of it. I'm paying my own way in New York City, and it feels pretty damn good.

We get out, and he follows me inside and up the stairs.

"Sorry, no fancy elevator here for your dirty talk," I say as he follows me up. I feel his hand graze my ass.

"Don't need an elevator for that," he whispers, and I giggle as he kisses my neck. We round the corner, and I'm fiddling with my keys and pull out the one to my apartment. He's got his arm around my neck, and he's kissing the side of my head as we walk down the long hall. I can't remember the last time I've felt so...okay. Like everything is in its place, and if it's not, it will be.

And then we reach my apartment, and my keys fall from my hand when the man at my door turns around.

"Dad," I say.

20

APRIL 2015 - MARYN

I'm lying on my bed, trying desperately to focus on my stupid math test tomorrow. I can't focus on a damn thing these days, yet somehow, I've just been going through the motions like everything's fine. My friends at school rarely even bring my dad up anymore, which is both a relief and also sort of pisses me off.

It's like he's been written off, written out of their lives. And yet, our lives are still stalled, waiting for someone else to decide when they can continue on again.

I roll onto my back and stare up at my ceiling when I hear them talking downstairs. Mom's voice is high, and I immediately spring up. That's either really good or really bad. And as my experience over the last few months has taught me, it's usually the latter.

I run to my bedroom door, open it, and trot down the stairs, Tucker in line behind me. I feel bad that he's going through this, too. He's only in eighth grade, and I think the whole distance from the high school thing is helpful, but I know it has to be eating away at him, too. He and my dad are extra close, and my dad is more of a shell of his old self than anything else these days.

"Mom? Dad? What's going on?" I ask as we get to the kitchen. Dad's nodding and repeating "okay" into the phone then thanks whoever he's talking to profusely before hanging up.

My heart's beating in my chest so hard that I feel it in my throat.

"Dad?"

He sighs and rubs his temples, and when he looks up at us, there are tears in his eyes.

"They've officially cleared me as a suspect," he says, his hand dropping to his side. "There was new video evidence discovered that shows I was still in the store when she was taken."

My mom shrieks and jumps on him, wrapping her arms around his neck and kissing him over and over.

"Thank *God!*" she cries, burying her face in his shoulder. "This nightmare is almost over!"

Dad hangs his head as he sets her back down to the floor.

"Hopefully, for us, it is. But for that family, it's just getting started," Dad says. I look up at my dad and narrow my eyes at him. Of course, it's absolutely devastating that the Mills family is back to square one. But right now, all I can think about is that my dad is *not* square one. He's no square at all, anymore, and there's a weight that's lifted off my shoulders with each passing moment.

I lean over and hug him, breathing in his comforting smell, holding on to him tight, and willing the old dad to come back now. *It's okay, Dad. We're gonna be okay.*

"So when can you come back to school?" I ask as he kisses the top of my head and ruffles Tucker's hair.

"I'm going to call Eduardo right now and find out," he says, grabbing his cell phone off the counter and walking up to his study. He's back down in a few minutes and smiles.

"The county called Eduardo and set up a meeting for us tomorrow," he says. "Let's go out to eat."

Tucker and I both perk up and run to the door to get our shoes. We haven't gone out for food since before this whole thing started. Mom said it was just easier; the less people that saw us, the more people would forget about Dad's involvement—or lack thereof—so we've been staying pretty incognito. We started doing our grocery shopping in the next town over and avoided all public get-togethers in general. I'm ready to get back into the Tilden life. I'm ready for my town to bring me that same warm, cozy feeling it always has. The one that says, "Relax. You're home."

We get to Jenny's, our favorite diner in the center of town, and my dad already seems like he's back to being his old self. He's smiling at the wait staff, and so far, nothing has reminded us of why it's taken us so long to get back here.

We're sharing a huge plate of fries when a family walks in and is seated at the booth adjacent to ours.

I'm not sure if it's just me being observant, or if it's the sensitivity to the subject I've come to acquire, but I feel their eyes on us over and over. Finally, I turn my head and make eye contact with the mother, who's staring at us with narrowed eyes.

She whispers something to her husband who also looks up at us. Her two kids, who I recognize from school, look over at us then look back down at their plates.

I stand up from the booth. My mother pulls on my hand, but I ignore her.

"Mare, sit down," Dad whispers. "Just ignore it."

But I'm done ignoring it. It's been too goddamn long. Too much bad press. Too many panned shots of our house on the news. Too many instances of my dad's name being dragged through the mud. Shit's getting old.

"Can we help you?" I ask, my voice loud and booming through the small diner. Everything around us gets eerily quiet. My mother ducks her head on the table, shielding her eyes. My father scoots closer to the edge of the booth, getting ready to pounce.

The woman at the table crosses her arms over her chest and leans back, rolling her eyes in my direction.

"No, I think your family has done quite enough to this town, thank you," she says, spinning around to unfold her napkin and lay it on her lap.

"Excuse me?" I say, feeling every inch of me begin to shake with anger.

"You heard me, girlie," she says.

"He had *nothing* to do with it," I say behind clenched teeth. "You'll be interested to know that he has officially been cleared as a suspect."

She looks past me, at my dad, then back to the table.

"Humph," she says. "I'll believe that when—"

"When what? When you hear it on TV? Real reliable," I say. "Do you know my dad? Has he taught your children?"

"No, thank goodness," she says.

"That's enough, Maryn, let it go," my dad says.

"Yeah, let it go," the woman says. She waves her

waitress over. "We'd like to change tables. I don't need my kids near this man."

The waitress looks back at us with shame in her eyes then nods her head and obliges. The woman leans in toward our table as they walk past.

"You might want to keep your own kids away from him, too," she says to my mother. I can't hold myself back. I lunge after her just as my dad stands up and wraps his arms around me, holding me back and squeezing me.

"Fuck you, lady!" I cry, and I hear my mother gasp.

Dad turns to our waiter.

"We'll take our food to go," he says, defeat in his voice.

My mother has tears streaming down her face, and Tucker is staring blankly ahead.

We shouldn't have come out.

I'm crying. Mom's crying. And Dad's seconds away from losing his shit.

We're in the car, driving home, and Dad reaches his hand back and squeezes mine.

"We're gonna be okay, kid," he says. I squeeze his hand back.

"They can't say things about you," I say, wiping the tears from my face. "They aren't true."

"I know, kid. I know. Truth is, they can say whatever they want. We just have the power not to listen," he says.

I nod and rest my head against my window.

The next day, I'm anxiously checking my phone in seventh period, waiting for the good news. I can't wait for Dad to get back to work. I can't wait for life to get back to normal. To shove it in all those people's faces who doubted him.

My phone buzzes, and I look down to see a message from Mom.

Call me when you're done.

No emoji, no smiley, nothing.

Not good.

I raise my hand and ask to go to the bathroom. I scurry out into the hall and dial her.

"What is it? When can he come back?" I ask before she can even say hello. Mom sighs into the phone.

"I'm coming to get you."

No. No, no, no, no. Not again. My stomach is turning and flipping on itself, making me feel queasier by the minute.

I walk back into my classroom and gather my books, dumping them into my backpack. I walk out of the room without saying a word, Mr. Patterson calling my name and staring after me as I walk away.

Mom signs me out again then grabs my bookbag and carries it to the car. She shuts the door, and I turn to her.

"When can he come back?" I ask her again.

She drops her head and pinches the bridge of her nose. Then, she looks up at me.

"He's not," she says.

"What?" I ask, my throat burning.

"The county called him in today to tell him that they can no longer employ him as a teacher," Mom says.

"H-how? He was cleared!"

"I know, hon. We all know. But they claim it's bad press for the county to have someone working with students who was involved in a case like this."

"But he *wasn't* involved! He was just going to the goddamn grocery store!" I cry out, the tears already streaming down my face. The sharp breaths I'm taking are burning my insides.

"I know, baby, I know," she says, and I see her lip trembling. "They've offered him an admin job at the central county office until the end of the school year. Then, he will need to find something else."

"What? *Fuck* that! He's a *teacher!* He wants to *teach!* This makes no sense. Who can we talk to? He didn't. Do. *Anything!*" I say, screaming now. Mom just lets me go. She lets me cry, tears streaming down both of our faces. She takes my hand after a moment and squeezes it.

"He's going to be okay," she says. "Don't worry. We will all be okay."

"We keep telling ourselves that," I say, "but what are we going to do? How can any of this be okay? He's cleared as a suspect, yet they *still* fired him? And what about Dad? He spends the rest of his life behind a desk? And then what? All he wants to do...all he *can* do is teach! How is this fair for anyone?"

"It's not, honey," Mom says. "It's not."

"So is he going to take the admin job?" I ask, wiping my nose on my sleeve.

"He doesn't have much of a choice," Mom says. "No other county will hire him right now. Not after this case. We need the money, and unfortunately, there's not much else he can do with a teaching degree. I'm hoping by the end of the school year, he can find something else."

I think for a minute.

"Let's move," I say. Mom lets out a chuckle and strokes my hair.

"Believe me, we've thought about it," she says. "But

I can't do that to Tucker. He's still in school; he's so young. His friends are here. We can't let them take away everything."

I nod, but it feels like they pretty much already have.

LATER THAT NIGHT, Dad's sitting on the reclining chair, scrolling on his laptop.

"Whatcha doing, Dad?" I ask gently, as if I'm going to startle him by speaking. He looks up at me for a moment, taking his glasses off to rub his eyes.

"My resume," he says, putting them back on. I raise an eyebrow.

"Are you applying for something else?" I ask.

He shakes his head.

"No. The county is making me reapply for that admin job," he says with a sigh. I nod slowly. Those fuckers. They already have all his information. He's worked for them for 25 goddamn years. Does he *really* need to go through all this?

I scoot closer to him and squeeze his hand. He stops typing for a minute and looks up at me.

"Didn't think that I'd be looking for a new career at fifty years old," he says with a sad chuckle.

"I know, Dad," I say, my voice cracking. "I'm so sorry. I wish there was something I could do."

He squeezes my hand back.

"I know, kid," he says, "but you've got to worry about you. You've got exams to worry about, graduation, and *college* to worry about. You've got so much ahead of you."

I nod. As much as I don't want to leave my family in a few months, I am actually really looking forward to college. I haven't had anything to look forward to in a while. I decided on Melladon, after all. It's the farthest away from all of this, and I know distance is just what I need.

I flip through the channels as Dad works away, but I stop when I see a new headline at the bottom of the news screen.

Body found in Meinhart could be missing Tilden girl.

21

WYATT

O h, fuck.

I haven't seen Mr. Porter in five years. Not since the day I saw him leaving a flower on Willa's grave.

He had looked so sad, and I remember feeling so guilty. He lost a student, one he actually cared about, after he got blamed for—and eventually cleared—for her abduction.

After he lost everything.

And now, he has that same look on his face. He doesn't look angry; he doesn't look mad. He looks really, really fucking sad. I let my arm slide off of Maryn's shoulders.

"Dad," she says, standing straight up and staring him right in the eyes. I can feel how fast her heart is racing just by standing this close to her. I'd never want to leave her, but right now, I think it would be better for all parties involved if I had the ability to vanish into thin air.

Mr. Porter doesn't say anything. He just drops his head and walks past us. She looks up to me.

"I'm sorry," she says, and I shake my head and hold my hand out.

"No, no, go, we'll catch up later," I say. I watch as she trails out after him, catching up to him as he jogs down the stairs. I stare at the apartment door in front of me. I've still never been inside.

Seeing the sadness in his eyes, it hits me with this wave of guilt.

My family and I…we went through hell. But I also ruined Mr. Porter's life, his reputation, his career in the process.

I can't blame myself. To this day, I know I was desperate. I know I was reaching for a reason, for someone to blame. And I know I had a pretty good excuse. But it wasn't him.

And now I'm on the verge of falling in love with his daughter.

Shit.

I walk back down the steps and pull my phone out of my pocket.

"Ma?" I say when she answers.

"Hey, hon," she says. "What are you up to?"

"Not a whole lot. Are you and Dad around? I was thinking of coming into town."

I can practically hear the smile on her face. I don't go home a lot. There's a lot of heaviness left there.

"Yep, we're home," she says, "and we would love to see you."

I TAKE a cab out to Tilden and pay the fare as I stare up

at my childhood house. Tilden was a good place to grow up. Everyone knew everyone; the streets were normally safe—until Willa. People didn't seem to care that my parents were an interracial couple, and the race issues that we heard about were never a real issue here for Willa and me.

But after she was gone, it felt like a totally different place to me. It didn't feel like home. It felt like the place my sister was taken from. It felt like a nightmare that I couldn't wake up from. My parents didn't feel the same. This house didn't feel the same. I didn't feel the same.

I take in a deep breath and make my way up the walk.

"Hey, boy," my dad says from his chair on the front porch. I almost didn't notice him. "Oh, hey, pop," I say. "Mom inside?"

"Nah, she ran up to the store to get some things for lunch. Not every day you come home to see us."

I scratch the back of my neck and sit down next to him.

"Yeah, I know, Dad. Sorry about that."

"Don't be sorry, boy. It doesn't have to be your home just because it's ours," he says. I nod. "So what brings you in today?"

I swallow. I'm not exactly sure why I'm home, but I know I came back for something. My dad leans forward, closer to me. He raises an eyebrow.

"What's eatin' you?" he asks. I smile. We might not be as close as we once were, but my dad still knows me.

"I'm sort of seeing this girl," I say nervously, like a teenage kid about to ask his dad about condoms or something. Dad smiles.

"Oh, really?" I nod. I take in a deep breath and rub

my hands down my knees. I guess now's as good of a time as any.

"Dad, I'm sort of seeing Maryn Porter," I say. I wait for the exasperation, the crazy look in his eyes, anything. But he pauses for a moment then nods his head.

"Well, alright then," he says, leaning back in his chair with a smile.

I'm staring at him blankly.

"'Alright, then'? That's it?" I say. He chuckles.

"What did you want me to say?"

I shrug.

"I don't know. I guess I just thought you'd have more of a reaction."

"I have no problem with the Porters, son, you know that," he says. "I'm not so sure they feel the same way."

This makes me laugh.

"You have no idea," I say, leaning back in my chair and rubbing my head. "Her dad caught us together today. He didn't look as, uh, laid back as you do about it."

My dad nods his head, and he scratches at his goatee.

"That man went through a lot," Dad says. I nod.

"Because of me."

Dad shakes his head.

"No, Wyatt, not because of you. Because of bad timing. And because you were just a boy trying to find his sister and would have done anything to bring her home."

My dad leans forward and squeezes my hand.

"Wyatt, if that happened again today, I'd expect you to do the same thing. We were all trying to be detectives, trying to look for the missing piece, trying to bring our girl home. You did what anyone would do. You saw that man, and you told the truth about it. And that's all there is to it."

I lean back in my chair and close my eyes, thinking back to that first night when I said his name at the precinct.

"He lost his job," I say, more to myself than him.

"He did," Dad says.

"His reputation went to shit," I say.

"It did," Dad says.

"And Willa still never came home."

Dad sits up again and leans into me, knocking me gently with his shoulder.

"No, son, she didn't."

I feel this tightness in my chest. I feel like a pot about to boil over. All these years, all this time, and I've never really talked to my parents about Willa. I've never really let it out. I've never gotten over my role in all of it.

"I miss her," I say, and my lip actually starts to quiver, like I'm a five year old. My dad scoots forward on his chair and wraps his big arms around me. His skin is the darkest it is all year round, and I know it's from his gardening. He pulls me in tight, and suddenly, I'm bawling on his shoulder.

"I do, too, Wyatt. We all do," he says. "But, son, it's not your fault. None of it."

I squeeze my eyes shut and bury my face into my father's shoulder.

"I should have gone inside with her, Dad. Why didn't I go inside?"

Dad lets me cry for a few more moments before pushing back and looking at me. His hands are on both of my shoulders, holding me steady.

"Because you never could have imagined the world could be so ugly, son," he says quietly. I catch my breath and nod my head. He's damn right about that.

We sit quietly for a little while, just rocking back and forth on the porch.

"What's she like?" he finally asks. I look over to him.

"Maryn? She's…" I think for a minute. God, what *isn't* she? "She's a lot of things I didn't know I was missing," I say, thinking about the way it felt to wake up to her this morning. I already can't wait to see her again. To watch her eyes light up when she sees food, or to hear her laugh in the office. To smell her hair again the next time she's in my bed. "She's tough. She doesn't beat around the bush. She loves her family pretty fiercely."

Dad's smiling.

"Well, all of that sounds like a pretty good choice," Dad says. I nod and look down at the ground. Her family. But like always, he reads my mind. "Son, her family will come around. You and this girl…you two need to worry about *you two*. No one else."

I nod, and we sit in silence again. Then Dad lets out a chuckle.

"What?"

"Nothin'. Just a crazy universe we live in that Maryn Porter and you found each other again."

I smile to myself. Yeah, it is crazy. But this time, I don't intend to ruin her life, or let her go.

22

MARYN

I feel like a kid that's been scolded, following my dad down the sidewalk with my tail tucked between my legs.

"Dad, please, just talk to me!" I finally call out after several other attempts to get his attention. We reach a park bench farther on the outskirts of the city, and he stops and takes in a deep breath. I see him close his eyes, then he sits down. He doesn't look at me or invite me to sit. He just stares blankly ahead at the river, blinking every so often.

"Wyatt Mills, Maryn? Wyatt *Mills?*" he asks, his voice coarse and low. I take a breath and sit next to him.

"Dad, look, it just sort of—"

"*Don't* say it just sort of happened, Maryn," he says, his tone harsh—way more harsh than I'm used to when it comes to him. "These things don't just happen. The police, the media taking a beating on me like they did just to buy some time...that doesn't just *happen*. It's calculated. When systems fail, it's easier to pin these things on one small person than it is to actually *fix* the goddamn system."

I swallow, a lump in my throat threatening to rise to the surface.

"I'm sorry, Dad."

"But you're seeing him anyway," my dad says, sort of like a question but more matter-of-factly. "Did you know he worked there before you took the job?"

I look down at my hands in my lap but don't answer. I don't have to.

"Jesus, Maryn. This is going to kill your mom," he says.

"We just made it official yesterday, Dad. I wasn't trying to hide it from you; I just needed some time to figure it out."

My dad turns to me slowly, and I see the pain behind his eyes. My heart rips in half.

"Maryn, do you remember what we lost? Do you remember the letters kids put in your locker, calling you the murderer's kid? Do you remember them cleaning out my classroom because I wasn't even allowed back in to get my things? Do you remember them hauling me off to the police station, month after month, just to answer the *same* questions over and over, just to throw me to the side once they couldn't use me anymore?"

Yes. Yes, I do remember it. All of it.

And yet somehow, inexplicably, Wyatt made me forget.

I look up to my dad, the tears prickling behind my eyes.

"You're right, Dad. It was selfish of me. I'm sorry," I say. My dad doesn't say anything else. He just nods.

Then, he takes a breath and stands up from the bench and walks away.

I sit on the bench for a few minutes and cry like an idiot, letting the fall air blow through my hair.

This next part is going to suck.

Because Wyatt and I have to end before we even got started.

I GET BACK to my apartment and collapse onto the couch. Ellie is still at work, so I reach for my phone and call Keely.

"Hey," she says, out of breath.

"Hey—what are you doing?" I ask.

"Sweating for the wedding, bitch," she says. "What's wrong with you?"

I smile. It's funny how friends, or—as her and Ellie are—soul sisters, just need a few syllables and they can guess your entire mood. A few syllables.

"My dad saw us," I mutter just as my voice cracks.

"Shit," she says, and I can hear her pressing a button in the background. The sound of the treadmill slows until I can tell she's off of it completely. "So, what happened?"

"I think I need to break it off," I say. I wait for her to interfere, to stop me, to push me to do what's best for me. But she takes a deep breath.

"Ya know, Mare," she says, "I've never met a family like yours, that would downright kill for one another the way the Porters would. You know I want you to be happy, and if that means being with Wyatt, then by all means, go ahead. I just… I can't truly *see* you being happy if your family isn't. It's not who you are. I mean, if your parents won't speak to him—or even you—could you live with that?"

I swallow and shake my head in silence.

"No," I finally croak out. "No, I couldn't."

She sighs.

"Damn, I'm really sorry, Mare. I know this was fun for you, but maybe it's a good thing he saw you two together now versus in a few months or something. At least you're not in too deep."

I open my eyes and stare up at the ceiling. That's just the thing.

I *am* in too deep. I think I was the second I saw him in that bar at Melladon. I thank her and tell her I love her then hang up.

I know I should call him, arrange a meet-up, end it now, and rip the bandage off. But I can't bring myself to do it. So I avoid it altogether by turning on *Ridiculousness* and stuffing my face with leftover pasta from last night. This oughta help.

My phone buzzes about an hour later, and it's him. I swallow as I set down my dish.

Hey, how did it go with your dad?

Ha.

Horrible. He hates your guts, and we can't see each other.

I sigh and text back. Then stop. Then text back again. Then stop.

Then I put my phone down and lie back on the couch. I can't do this.

A few hours later, I wake to a knock on my door. It's gentle, but it's enough to startle me awake. Ellie's still not home yet, and she has a key. So I know who it is before I even go to the door. I drag myself from the couch and sulk over, looking through the peephole. Ugh. Even distorted and the size of a dime, he's freakin' beautiful. His eyes are gleaming emeralds in the harsh hallway light, and his skin is brown and delicious. I sigh and drop my forehead to the door. Then, I take a breath and open it up.

I stare up at him, and his expression goes from excited and hopeful to downright disastrous in a matter of seconds. He's holding some sort of carryout bag and two sodas. I stand back and let him come in.

"I thought the lack of a response wasn't a good sign," he says as he sets his things down on the coffee table, "and your expression doesn't exactly make me feel better." He gives a sad smile and stuffs his hands in his pockets.

God, he's beautiful.

I smile back at him and motion for him to sit down.

"So," he says, keeping a noticeable distance between us on the couch, "what did he say?"

I sigh again before looking up at him nervously.

"He didn't have to say much to know that I broke his heart," I say. Wyatt's eyes sink to the floor. "It's just that he went through so much—we all did—and I think there are parts of him that never recovered. And seeing us together made him realize those parts that are still missing."

Wyatt nods, and I feel that lump in my throat.

"So, what did you tell him about us?" he asks. I swallow a few times, trying desperately to win this no-cry battle.

I stare down at my hands.

"I can't hurt him any more, Wyatt," I whisper. "I

can't see you. I can't be with you if it's going to tear my family up. I won't hurt them more."

I finally muster up a bit of courage and look up to him. He's still staring down at the ground, but he's nodding his head.

"I understand," he says, rubbing his hands up and down on his thighs. "I was hoping that time would heal some of this, but I know it can't heal all. It certainly hasn't for me. I can't expect it to for him, either."

I nod slowly. Then, he pushes himself to stand, and I feel my heart sink in my stomach.

He makes his way toward the door slowly. I jump to my feet, feeling panic taking over. I know he needs to go. I know this has to end here. My head knows. But some other part of me is screaming to hold on. To jump on him and not let him go.

"Wyatt," I say, just as his hand is landing on the door handle.

He half-turns to me, raising his eyebrows.

"This all…" I say, motioning between the two of us. "This all meant something to me. More than I bargained for." I take a few steps closer to him.

He smiles that sad smile again, hanging his head and turning toward me.

"For me, too," he says, barely above a whisper. "More than you know." He looks up at me, and all it takes is one quick connection, for our eyes to meet, for me to start forgetting it all again.

I launch myself forward so that our chests slam together, pushing his back up against the door. I cover his lips with mine, tasting him, taking him all in. I wrap my arms tightly around his neck, pulling him into me as closely as possible. It takes him a moment, but then I feel his arms snake around my back. He shifts so that he can lift me up, letting my legs wrap around his waist. He pushes off the door and into the apartment more, swirling us around. Our tongues are intertwining, our lips crashing into each other desperately. He carries me to the other side of the apartment, placing me on top of our breakfast bar. I reach my hands down to tug on the hem of his shirt. I lift it slightly, and I can practically feel the warmth of his familiar chest before I even lift it past his belly button. I need him, to be pressed up against him, my skin on his, feeling it all.

But he reaches his hands down and grabs mine, stopping me. He tears his lips from mine, both of us heaving with heavy breaths, and rests his forehead against mine.

"Maryn," he whispers, and I know I'm not going to like what comes next. I reach my hands up around his neck, pressing us harder together, hoping I get him to shut up and kiss me again. "Maryn," he says again, unlocking my hands from his neck and kissing them. "I can't do this."

I close my eyes for a moment, letting his words hit me like a ton of bricks. Then, I open them and stare into his.

"I'm sorry," he says, "but it's going to make it harder not to do it again. And again. And again. We can't do this. Not if we need to be apart."

And those last few words are all it takes for my heart to crumble to dust in my chest. He takes a step closer to me, forcing my legs apart slightly. He wraps an arm around my waist, pulling me into him, and the other hand around my head.

He kisses my jaw softly then my lips. He presses his

lips to my forehead one last time then to the top of my head. He squeezes me gently then slowly pulls himself away from me.

"I'm going to miss the idea of you being mine," he says with that same sad smile.

"The idea of it?" I ask. He nods.

"I never even got to take you on a real date," he says as he gets closer and closer to the door.

"Wyatt, I *was* yours," I whisper as the tears form in my eyes. He drops his head again then pulls on the door handle and disappears. And the tears start flowing down my cheeks, because I know that I still am.

23

APRIL 2015 - WYATT

There's this blinking light in the vending machine in front of me, and I am staring at it like a bug with a porch light. Overall, this is probably the saddest looking vending machine I've ever seen. The contents are sparse; the only section that's still full is the fig bars—because no one goes to a vending machine with the intention of grabbing one of those—and almost everything else is empty. Plus, I know now, from watching three different people insert coins, that it no longer takes money. It spits them back out with impressive force. It's almost like it's just standing here, waiting to die, not wanting to be bothered. Right now, I have more in common with this vending machine than I care to admit.

"Come on back," I hear Detective Robinson say, his voice hushed. I turn my head slowly to his office door.

Oh, that's right.

We're here because they think they found my sister's dead body.

He leads us down a dark corridor, and I find it ironic

that the lights are so spread out. It's like every scary movie you've ever seen that has a scene in a morgue.

My parents are a few paces ahead of me, my mom shaking vigorously as my dad tries to steady her. We reach the door with the damning "MORGUE" sign on it, and we all stop.

"Do you all want to go in?" Detective Robinson asks. Mom's nodding her head as little sobs shake her body. My dad grumbles out a "yes" but turns to me.

"Son, do you want to wait out here?" he asks.

I think about it for a moment because, yes, the idea of seeing my sister's dead body isn't exactly on my list of things I want to do today.

But I know that if I don't, I'll regret it. I'll regret it because if I don't see it with my own eyes, I won't believe it. I'll always doubt everyone else. Not that I have much faith in myself these days, but as sickening as it is, I need the visual confirmation.

I'm a grown man. I can handle this.

I nod, and Detective Robinson nods back. He takes a deep breath then slowly pushes open the big, heavy door to the morgue. The room is freezing. I see the drawers against the back wall, and it sends a chill down my spine.

Like a goddamn horror movie.

There's a stretcher in the middle of the room, covered in a white sheet. Now that I think about it, everything in this goddamn room is white.

So white it's making my head hurt. I'm sick to my stomach.

We walk toward the table, and Detective Robinson takes a deep breath before reaching for the sheet. He looks up at us.

"Are you ready?" he asks.

We nod, Mom squeezing her eyes shut.

Then, he lifts the sheet.

Mom screams, stumbling backward as Dad catches her. Detective Robinson is grabbing her other arm, helping Dad steady her.

And me… I'm staring at my sister's dead body. Before I realize it, I'm on my knees on the ground. I put my hands out to steady myself, but the whole room is spinning. Why is *everything* so goddamn *white?*

Someone else comes into the room carrying a small cup of water for Mom. They are ushering her out, and someone's calling for a chair.

But I'm still here, kneeling below my sister's body. Her lips were puffy and had a hint of purple. Her cheeks were taut and narrow. But aside from the bruised handprints around her neck, she looked the same. The same as the night I let her go into that store.

God, why is *everything* in this room white?

Everything around me is spinning again, then I feel the burning in my stomach as it erupts. I puke all over the floor in front of me, blinking back as my eyes water. Someone comes in and pulls me up, and then I hear the rolling of a mop bucket a few seconds later.

I'm pulled out into the hallway, and they slump me into a chair. Detective Robinson is kneeling down in front of me when I finally open my eyes. He's holding out a small plastic cup of water.

"I'm sorry, Wyatt," he whispers. Then, he stands up, cupping his chin with his hand and shaking his head. "I'm so, so sorry."

Then, he walks away. I turn down the hall and see my parents making their way toward the door, being escorted by a larger policeman who is, no doubt, there for catching purposes in case my mother drops again.

I take in a few deep breaths, staring at the big "MORGUE" door right in front of me.

My sister is dead.

24

WYATT

It's been almost two weeks since I walked out of her apartment, and they've been the longest, slowest two weeks of my life.

My days have consisted of working myself out so hard at the gym that I want to faint, working my ass off so hard at work that my eyes are crossing, and then collapsing onto my bed at the end of the night, feeling like I've accomplished nothing.

And then I picture her, or her face pops up in my email address book, and it's all I can do not to get off on the thought of her.

In fact, a few times, late at night, when I'm in the shower or lying in my bed, there *has* been nothing I could do to stop myself.

I think of her naked. I think of her half-naked. I think of her fully-fucking-clothed, smiling and laughing as we got pizza or drinks, or as she stuck her fork into my Chinese food.

I think of how I could talk about Willa so easily with her. How I didn't feel like I had to hide that part of my life, because she already knew about it. I think about how she made me want to go back to Tilden, be a part of the town that made me.

But it's too good to be true. Because our lives collided all those years ago and were never meant to cross again.

I'm sitting at my desk on a rainy Tuesday afternoon, clicking away at a pen while I stare at my screen. I'm supposed to be presenting at a staff meeting this afternoon, but I'm feeling less than inspired. Plus, I could school these guys with something I pull out of my ass five minutes before the meeting, so there's not much riding on it.

I hear laughter in the hall, and when I look up, my balls feel like they're sucking up into my stomach.

She's walking down the hallway with Nate, laughing at something he's said. They're headed for the elevators, and my head is pounding with jealousy, curiosity, and a little bit of suspense.

I grab for my coffee mug for a fake refill and hop up so that I'm landing in the hall just as they're passing my office.

"Hey, guys," I say, keeping my voice as casual as possible. I feel her icy blue eyes lift up to me then back down. Nate nods his head back and gives me a look.

And now that I think about it, we haven't talked much in the last few weeks. And that stirs all these emotions up just a little bit more.

"Hey, man," he says quietly, lifting the strap of his laptop case up higher on his shoulder.

"You guys headed out?"

"Uh, yeah," he says, running the back of his fingers against his chin. "Another quick lunch meeting." I nod. He's not giving up anything, and by the way she's avoiding eye contact with me, I can tell she won't either. "We actually have to get going so we're not late. We'll catch up later, yeah?"

I nod and smile, watching her for a moment too long before they disappear into the elevators.

I get back to my desk without even bothering to complete the charade of getting another cup of coffee and pull up their calendars again. Blocked. I bet it's that fucking gallery. What *is* this client? Why is there no record of it?

I let the questions fester in my mind all damn day until I hear the ding of the elevator a few hours later. They get off, carry-out cups in hand again, laugh about a few more things, and then go their separate ways.

Time for another fake refill.

I grab my mug again and move toward the door, heading for the kitchen that's on the other side of her cube. I pause at her desk and clear my throat.

She looks up at me.

"Hi," she says, her voice quiet. But her eyes have this pleading look to them, like she wants me to say more than just "hi" back. On the corner of her desk is a stack of paperwork she's just dropped down—entitled "Eloway Gallery."

Eloway. Mark that down to search the shit out of later.

"Hey. How was your meeting?" I ask her. She smiles and nods.

"It went well," she says. "How are you?"

I smile and tilt my head a bit. She doesn't mean

how's my work. She means how am *I*. Like, how am I holding up since I forced myself to leave her panting and clawing at me a few weeks earlier. God, I'm a stupid, stupid man.

I shrug. And then I'm hit with a steaming pile of honesty.

"I feel like I felt a few months ago, before I made this trip down to my college town," I say. She cocks an eyebrow at me. "I feel like life's on track, things are going as they should." Her eyes narrow at me. "Except that it always feels like something's missing. But now, different than before, I know what that something is."

I don't know why I say it. I don't know how it comes out so smoothly, but it does. She's staring at me with her mouth open the slightest bit, and I tap on her desk and walk by, this time actually getting that second cup of coffee.

I take the long way around to get back to my office so that I don't have to pass her.

I get what she needs. I get why it's complicated. I get why it's probably damned and probably never going to amount to anything. But I need her to know what she meant—what she *means*—to me. The truth is, I'm not okay. And for the first time in my life, I don't feel like I have to pretend to be.

I get back to my computer and immediately search for "Eloway Gallery." And for the first few scrolls, there's close to nothing about this damn place. I go to the second or third page of results, and then, finally, I see something—Eloway Gallery mentioned in an online chatroom of sorts.

There's not a ton of information aside from one of the people claiming to be in charge of it. Lots of good merchandise supposed to be available from all over the world, hoping to be in operations within the year.

Then, finally—bingo—a location. I jot down the address on a piece of paper just as Rex is making his way into my door.

"How's my star?" he asks, grabbing a mint off my desk and tearing into the wrapper with his teeth. He balls it up and throws it at the wastebasket next to my desk and, per usual, misses. And also, per usual, he never bends over to pick it up. Once, he made a comment to me that he pays people to clean the office for him, so it's useless to do their job for them. But every time he leaves, I bend over and pick up his damn trash.

"Hey, Rex," I say, quickly clearing out of the browser and covering up the address. "Doing well. How are you?"

"Great. Just heard from Landry, and they are really happy with the first month's results. Great presentation you sent over," he says. I smile and nod. Luckily, our first analytics presentation was due to Landry last week, so I've been able to stay focused—for the most part—at work on that.

Unless she walks by in those form-fitting skirts, or those godforsaken dress pants, or the blouses that tie at the front.

Shit. Unless she walks by, period.

Then, I'm a puddle of useless mush.

"Good, I'm glad. I'm really happy with the first month. Hoping to beat the numbers this month," I say. He smiles and nods.

"Thatta boy. You ready for today's presentation?" he asks. I nod and give him my best grin.

"Always, sir," I say. He pats my shoulder and heads toward the door.

"That's why you're my number one," he says, holding up a finger as he walks out of my door. I gather my stuff for the meeting and scrape the piece of paper with the address on it into my briefcase. I have a pitstop to make after work today.

The meeting goes by swimmingly, just like I knew it would, with the board members clapping me on the back and asking all sorts of engaged questions. Nate sat at the back of the table with his arms crossed over his chest and a tight smile on his lips the whole time.

When the meeting ended, I grabbed my shit from my office and headed out.

I give the cabbie the address to the gallery, and after what feels like for-fucking ever, he drops me off between two buildings that I know are not in the best neighborhood. I thank him and pay the fare then get out and stare at the tattered building ahead of me. There's a sign on the front that says "Gallery" with an arrow pointing toward the alley. Of course there's an alley.

I follow it down to a red door on the side of the building and push it open. The inside smells musty but definitely looks like it could eventually be some sort of gallery. There's a few paintings already hanging, but other than that, though, nothing is set up yet. There's a counter, and as I take a few steps across the creaky wood floor, a tall, skinny dude pops up. He has long hair pulled back into a ponytail and a piercing in his eyebrow.

"Hey, can I help you?" he asks. I clear my throat, not exactly knowing what I'm here for.

"Uh, yeah, hi," I say. "I'm Wyatt. I'm a colleague of Nate Calloway's."

The man nods at me, then his lips break out into a smile. He shoves a hand at me.

"Hey, man, good to meet you," he says. "I'm Mack Teller. Nate and I went to high school together." I nod. Another rich boy, then. "So you're working on the deal, too?"

I nod slowly as I shake his hand.

"Well, sort of. He wants to bring me in on it but wanted me to come take a look at things ahead of time."

He nods slowly then holds his arms out.

"Well, here it is," he says. "We should be getting the rest of the artwork within the next few months. This room over here is going to be the lounge area, and then over in that corner is where we will sign the contracts."

I nod and look around. Nothing about this is raising any alarms, which is ticking me off. I know something's got to be going on here. I know it.

"So, have you decided on which services you'll be using Caldell for?" I ask, turning back to him. He leans back on his heel and cocks an eyebrow.

"Have Nate or Maryn not, uh, gone over everything with you?" he asks me, and I feel hot under my collar, like I'm about to blow my cover.

And the mention of her name makes me feel all clammy; it feels like she's in on something that she shouldn't be.

"We haven't exactly had a moment in private to go over the details," I say with a casual smile, "so he gave me the address and asked me to come here. He told me it was a private deal until things were worked out."

I pull a business card out of my wallet and hand it to him so he can see I am who I say I am.

He nods.

"So you know her, then?" he asks, leaning back against the counter.

"Maryn?" I ask, feeling that heat rising again. "Yeah, I know her from around the office. Although, he hasn't really explained her involvement with all this."

Mack nods as he walks around the counter, pulling a folder out from underneath a pile of other junk. He slaps it on the counter in front of me.

"So, we are going to be a specialty art gallery, definitely," Mack says. "But we will also be running another operation of sorts out of here."

He raises an eyebrow at me. I nod slowly to let him know I'm following, though I am most definitely not.

"We need some funding to get the place up and rolling—at least the art side of it—before we can bring in the behind-the-scenes operations. That's where Caldell comes in."

He opens the folder and pulls out some paperwork with the Caldell logo on it. It looks like a term agreement—like the ones that we provide all of our clients when we are ready to finalize an agreement with them. Except this isn't a term agreement; it's a sponsorship agreement.

"Wait, so you're not actually using Caldell for communications purposes?" I ask, staring down at the paperwork in front of me that has Maryn's signature all over it.

Mack gives me a look then chuckles.

"I mean, who knows. If the gallery takes off down the line, we very well could use ya for that. But Caldell sponsors and provides financial aid to startup businesses each year. This year, Eloway Gallery is going to be one of those businesses. It will help get the gallery front up and more substantial so that the, uh, underground stuff can flourish in the background."

Mack is all too comfortable and proud of himself for someone that just explained that he's launching an illegal drug ring.

I swallow as I stare down at the paperwork.

"And what exactly does Caldell get from this?" I ask, my voice low and filling with anger. Mack swallows nervously, noticing my tone.

"Uh, the satisfaction of pushing a small business forward," he says with a too-confident smile that makes me want to punch him in his entitled fucking face.

"And what does Nate get?" I ask.

"He's a sort of shareholder, ya know, of the behind-the-scenes business. He will get a cut."

I swallow again, my grip on the paperwork tightening.

"And Maryn?" I ask.

Mack gives me half a smile and shrugs.

"Someone's name had to be on the paperwork," he says. "Couldn't be Nate's, you know, just in case."

I nod slowly as my thumb grazes her signature on the paperwork in front of me.

"So, she has no idea?"

Mack shakes his head.

"I imagine not. It would be pretty hard to convince someone from the company to sign these and risk all that. We figured the new girl fresh into this fabulous corporate world would be a good one to go with."

He's so casual that it actually does take me a

moment to restrain myself. I want to slam his fucking head into the stupid granite counter in front of him.

But this isn't even his fault.

It's Nate's.

And now Maryn will take the fall for it.

I force myself to keep my cool, letting him know we would be in touch and that the deal sounded good. I have to keep myself looking like I'm truly working with Nate and not like I'm off to strangle him with my bare hands.

I hail a taxi outside, my hands squeezing into fists of anger.

Maryn trusted him. We all did.

I dial Rex on my cell, my hands shaking.

"Hey, Rex," I say, barely letting him get a word in. "Are you still at the office? I need to speak with you."

"Yep, still here. Come on by."

"I'll be there in about twenty." I hang up, resting my head back against the seat and willing all other cars in Manhattan to get the fuck out of the way.

As we're getting closer and closer to the office, I text Maryn.

Are you still at work? I ask.

I wait. Then wait a little bit more. But there's no response.

When we finally get to Caldell's block, I duck out of the cab, chucking cash back at the driver and basically sprinting back into the building. Nate will not do this. He won't use her. He won't hurt her, crush her spirit and her hard work.

She won't go through something like this. Not again.

The elevator seems painfully slow today, and my palms are sweaty against my sides. Finally, I hear that ding, and I run off. I make a mad dash down the hall toward Rex's office. Only, as I'm passing the cubicles, I see hers is empty. I have a sinking in my stomach as I keep walking, not acknowledging another human that I see.

I reach Rex's office just as he's holding the door open for Maryn. She has her head down to the ground. Nate's standing outside of his own office door, not the slightest bit of shame in his eyes. Fuck. Mack must have tipped him off. And suddenly, I see red.

"Rex," I say, breathless. He looks up at me.

"I'm sorry, Wyatt, but this'll have to wait. I have to speak with Maryn, here," he says, dismay in his voice and his eyes. I shake my head.

"Sir, I just need a minute. It's about this—"

"Not now, Wyatt." Then Rex closes the door, and Maryn disappears behind it. I clench my fists and storm into Nate's office where he's casually straightening out piles of paperwork on his desk

"How the fuck dare you," I grumble, slamming his door shut behind me. I hear gasps from outside as the sound made the whole building jump. Nate turns to me slowly, his eyes narrowed.

"Excuse me?"

"I didn't stutter. You were just going to have her slap her name on things, make her think she was taking a step up, but really you were setting her up."

Nate smiles, and I want to punch his teeth into his fucking brain.

"If she was dumb enough to screw you, I knew she'd be dumb enough not to suspect anything," he says, casually taking a sip from his coffee mug on the corner of his desk. I take a step toward him and swat the mug out of his hand, sending coffee everywhere. He barely acknowledges it, barely even lifts a brow.

"What did you say?" I ask.

"You heard me, Wyatt. Don't get all high and mighty. It doesn't take a genius to see the world's strongest case of sexual tension. And the way she can never stop talking about you pretty much gives it up," he says. For a short moment, I'm blinking like a madman, taking in his last few words. She thinks about me as much as I think about her. "Besides, Ricky saw you guys together, getting pizza, a few weeks ago." *Fuck.*

"Fuck you, Nate. She has nothing to do with this, and she's done nothing but everything you asked since she started."

He smiles again, dabbing at the coffee stain on his shirt with a tissue.

"Thus why I knew she'd be perfect," he says. "If I hadn't known that you'd already tainted her, I'd probably have requested a quick blowie in my office now and then. And you know what? She's *such* a good worker, I bet she would have obliged."

I stare at the man in front of me in a combination of disbelief and the purest anger I've ever felt.

Well, *almost* the purest anger. The only time I can remember wanting to kill someone so viciously was when I saw my sister's killer in the courtroom. This is a close second.

I lunge at him before my brain can catch up with my body's reaction, and before I know it, my fists are swinging in his direction. I land one to his chin just as the chair behind him is falling. He lands one to my gut, making me heave before I swing again, clocking him on his cheekbone. I stand up and grab him by his collar, shaking him and throwing him to the ground.

"She won't go down for this," I growl at him as he rubs his face.

"What, and you think I will? I'm the future face of this company. We both know I'm not going anywhere."

I glare at him before storming out of his office and back in the direction of Rex's. I have to fix this, because there's a fear in me that Nate's right.

I walk toward Rex's office, expecting to have to pound on the door, but to my surprise, it's open. I turn my head and see Priscilla walking Maryn toward her desk. Maryn's crying. I storm into Rex's office and slam the door shut.

"She didn't do it, Rex," I say.

Rex is sitting in his desk chair, his back to me, facing the crazy panoramic view of the city he has from his office. He's got his face in his hand.

"Rex," I say again. "She had nothing to do with this. She had no idea. It was...it was Nate."

Rex doesn't say anything. He just turns his chair around slowly. He takes in a deep breath then finally raises his eyes to me.

"I know," he whispers, rubbing the bridge of his nose.

"You...you know?" I ask. Rex is a good man. He's got a lot more integrity than his asshole son. But that doesn't explain why Maryn was crying.

Rex looks up at me, shame in his eyes.

"We both know he can't go down for something like this," Rex whispers. I swallow.

"What?" Rex is a good leader. A strong leader. I know he has more in him than this.

"Wyatt, he's my *son*," Rex says. "This is going to break soon. We got a tip from a friend in the police department that they've been tracking the gallery for a few months and believe they have eyes on their first shipment of drugs. And when it blows open, the names of every person and company involved will be exposed— including Caldell."

I'm staring at him.

"Rex, you *know* she had no idea," I plead, sitting down across from him at his desk. "Don't do this to her."

He shakes his head, letting out another long, slow breath.

"She's a good kid. But he's my son. I can't let our name go down with something like this. This will ruin his future. Maryn was at the wrong place at the wrong time, Wyatt."

I push myself up from the desk, clasping my hands behind my head as I walk to the window.

She's here partially because of me. She's here because she's a hard worker. She signed those papers because she thought she was doing her job.

I spin back to Rex.

"Say I did it," I say. His eyes flash to mine.

"What?"

"Say I was her manager, and I instructed her to sign that paperwork," I say.

Rex waves me off as he spins around in his chair like he's too afraid to face me head-on.

"I'm resigning today, Rex. Write up the press release, slap my name on it, and take her off of everything."

Rex's eyes are wide. He stands up now.

"Wyatt, you didn't have anything to do with it," he says.

"Neither did she. I'll sign an NDA. I'll sign whatever the fuck you want as long as it's written into the agreement that her name is kept out of it. That she had *no* voluntary involvement in it whatsoever. And she gets out from under him. He's no longer her manager."

I swallow. I know all that I'm about to throw away, and yet, there's not an ounce of fear in me. I can't undo her pain from all those years ago. I can't fix things for my sister. But I can fix this. At least for her.

"Wyatt, I…"

"Print up the agreement, Rex. Or I walk out that door and walk right to the nearest news station."

Rex drops his head, realizing his defeat. He nods to me slowly, and I spin on my heel and walk out of his office door. I walk into mine and start grabbing my things, throwing them into a box I have on my shelf. I see Rex walking out to Priscilla, then she makes her way to Maryn and whispers something to her.

Maryn's eyes flick up toward my office immediately, and I tuck myself back inside. I hear her coming as I'm shutting down my computer, the realization of unemployment setting in.

"Wyatt," she says quietly at my door. I look up at her. She looks confused and scared, and all I want to do is hold her.

"Hey," I say, trying not to sound as completely flustered as I feel. "Listen, I know you got into something you didn't understand. But everything is going to be okay, okay?"

She takes a step closer to me. I know she doesn't know what I mean, but she doesn't have to. As long as this doesn't ruin her, as long as she stays happy…that's all I need.

"Wyatt, what did you—"

I cut her off by touching her arm.

"It's gonna be okay," I tell her again before giving her the warmest smile I have to offer. Then, I gently push past her and make my way to the elevator.

25

MARYN

I've never felt such a whirlwind of emotions before. To go from being so scared, to so devastated when I thought my career was over, to being elated that I got my job back within a matter of minutes was giving me serious whiplash.

But then, he walked out of the building with all his shit in boxes, and I'm back to that sinking, devastating, scared feeling.

Within a matter of minutes, I went from being totally blindsided by the fact that my boss is a conniving, scheming asshole, to discovering that I was going to be fired for *his* illegal activity, then being told "Nevermind, you're all good. Take a seat and keep working."

As I walked out of Rex's office, crying, all heads were turned to me, and all noise had ceased.

Then, everyone's eyes turned to Wyatt as he left Caldell without saying goodbye to anyone.

Then, Priscilla helped me unpack the things I had already packed, and now I'm just sitting here while everyone pretends like this is a normal fucking day. I stand up from my desk a few minutes later and walk toward the front desk. Priscilla looks up at me, her whitish-blondish hair a little unkempt today, no doubt from the stressful orders she's been receiving and un-receiving over the last few hours.

"Priscilla?" I ask.

She looks up from her computer over the rim of her glasses.

"Yes, dear?"

"Is Wyatt gone because of me?" I ask her straight up. She swallows and looks around, making sure that none of the higher-ups are within listening distance.

"Not because of you," she says in a hushed tone. "But he is gone. He resigned today."

I swallow.

He resigned, and then I was told I got to keep my job.

He resigned so that I wouldn't be fired.

He's taking the heat for me.

I nod slowly and go back to my desk, somehow feeling worse than I did an hour ago when I discovered I had unknowingly signed documents to be used to fund a drug operation. Ha. I should throw *that* on my resume.

I pack up my bag and throw it over my shoulder, heading for the doors a few minutes early. Yet, after the day I've had, no one seems to care.

I should really call someone—my parents, my friends—but the only person I want to talk to is him.

I wave for a cab and give them his building address. And then I sit in silence in the backseat, staring out my window, not knowing if this is the right move or the absolute most wrong. All I know is, I need to see him.

I take a deep breath outside as I stare up at his

window then force myself through the big doors. I press the elevator button gently, like I'm not confident that I should be pressing it at all. When the doors open and I walk down the hall to his door, I feel my stomach swarm with butterflies, my hands clammy, my breathing rushed. I knock lightly three times. It takes him a moment, but then he's there, pulling the door open slowly, peering down at me with those big green eyes that make me lose my fucking mind.

"Hi," I say sheepishly, internally panicking because I'm not quite sure why I'm here, now that I'm... well...here.

"Hi," he says, leaning his arm up against the door over his head. He's wearing baggy sweats and a t-shirt, and I want to rip them off.

"I wanted to check on you," I say with a shrug. He nods and opens the door wider to let me in.

He closes the door slowly and welcomes me into the apartment.

"Well, thanks," he says, shrugging and stuffing his hands in his pockets. We stare at each other for a moment, then both of our eyes fall to the ground, both of us not knowing what to say. I look up at him again, soaking in how he looks, soaking in what he did for me today, and I'm overcome by this urge. I picture myself running to him, throwing myself on him...wait, no, I'm *actually* doing those things.

I jump up and wrap my arms around his neck, burying my face in his shoulder. I feel his thick arms curve up, wrapping around my back and lifting some of my weight. We stand still for a moment, just holding each other, and I haven't felt this good in weeks.

"I can't believe you did that for me," I whisper, not

wanting to be in his line of view as I say it. He sets me down slowly then tilts my chin up with his finger.

"You did nothing wrong," he says, "and you shouldn't have had to take the blame for it."

I feel tears prickling at my eyes again, because I feel so many things. Gratefulness toward him. Sadness that I won't see him every day. Anger with Nate. *Love* for the beautiful man in front of me.

"Neither did you, Wyatt," I say, realizing that my hands are still entwined around his neck.

He realizes it at the same time I do, because he reaches up and slowly unhooks them.

"What will you do now?" I ask. He shrugs and smiles, walking around behind the breakfast bar to put something away.

"I'll figure it out," he says. "Not sure I'll be able to find anything right away until this all blows over."

Oof. This hits home.

"Wyatt, I…"

He looks up at me and smiles, and I feel a tingle all over.

"Hey," he says. "Don't. I'm okay. I'll be okay. Just keep your head on right and keep working. You're doing a great job. They're going to move you out from under him. You'll get a small promotion. Not sure who your new manager will be, but no doubt it will be someone better. Just keep working. And keep your eyes peeled for another opportunity and another company. You deserve better."

I swallow and nod. I want nothing more right now than to grab him again, hold on to him, let him feel how much what he's done means to me. I can feel him trying to fix our past, trying to mend old wounds by stopping these new ones before they form. But what he doesn't get is that *he* is an old wound for me. One I'm not sure I want to heal if it means I can't have him.

I walk slowly around the breakfast counter and look down at his hands, pulling a few things out of grocery bags. I set my hand on top of his busy one, and he looks down at me again.

I'm looking for words. Something to tell him, something to build him up, like I did for Dad while he was going through everything. Things I told myself that I wasn't quite sure if I believed. But nothing's there. So I push myself against him and pull his lips to mine. He steps back for a moment, breaking us apart, and I swallow. I'm breaking the rules that I set for us.

But he looks down at me then wraps his fingers through my hair and pulls me into him again. I lock my arms around his neck and let my lips do all the talking for me. I kiss him hard, my tongue on his, pulling him into me as close as possible. He bends down and lifts me onto his kitchen counter, sitting me in front of him.

He gently tugs my hair back so that my head tilts up to him, and he pauses for a minute to look into my eyes. His eyes are searching my face, no doubt for the answers I'm not able to give him, then he kneels down to kiss me again. He cups my face in his hands, stopping every now and then just to look at me, and I can't remember a time when I've felt this close to someone.

He tilts my head back further then kisses my neck, and I feel a tingle zip through my body and park itself right between my legs. I moan and scoot myself closer to the edge of the counter so that I can wrap my legs around his waist.

As I grind myself onto him, he pulls away, his eyes widening. He looks down at me, his eyes hooded.

"Maryn…" he says, but I reach up and take his bottom lip in my teeth.

"Shh," I say when I let go. "Not tonight. Just let me have you."

His eyes are moving frantically between mine, and then he makes his decision. He slides his hands down my body and under my ass, picking me up and letting me wrap my whole body around his. He carries me into his bedroom and kicks the door shut behind us.

He takes a detour before we get to his bed, and he pushes me up against the wall. I squeeze my legs around him, feeling how hard he is and letting it drive me wild. He pulls my hair back and kisses my neck more, and I lean my head back against the wall, not sure I can support my own movements anymore.

I slide my hands down and tug his shirt off, throwing it to the ground. Then, I hold my arms above my head and let him do the same. He lets his fingers slide around my back and unclasp my bra, and I shiver as it slides down off of me. He moans as he takes my breasts in, sucking and nipping at them until I feel a pool between my legs.

He carries me to the bed and lays me back gently, sliding back down my body to pull my pants down. The anticipation is enough to make me explode in place, but I don't. I know what's waiting for me, and damn, I know it's worth waiting for. He pushes himself back then slides his sweats and boxers down and steps out of them.

There's something about seeing him completely naked that's dumbfounding to me no matter how many times I see it. It's like seeing him at his most glorious and his most vulnerable all at the same time, and it does inexplicable things to me.

I buck my hips in his direction, letting him know, letting him see how badly I need him. His eyes narrow at me, and he stalks toward me. I'm reaching up for him, and as soon as I can grab a hold of him, I pull him down to me. He rests on his elbows above me and strokes the side of my head with his thumb for a moment as he peers down at me.

"Maryn," he whispers.

"Hmm?"

"I'd go down for you a million times," he whispers. I close my eyes as his lips close in on mine, letting his words and kisses wash over me. God, I'd go down for him again, too. Any time, any where. His words lie above us in the air that's thick with our breaths, because I know what he's saying. And it's a hell of a lot more than what he's saying out loud.

He moves his hips back and parts me with his core-rattling size.

"Jesus, Wyatt," I moan, digging my nails into his brown skin. He's groaning above me, moving in and out of me in tantalizing, tortuous motions. But as he's thrusting in and out of me, I feel myself getting too close, too fast. I push back on him, and he pauses for a moment to make sure I'm okay. I grab his arms and swing him around, pressing him down onto the bed. I straddle him and slide onto him, and I watch as his eyes roll back into his head as he rests his hands on my hips. I move back and forth on top of him, and he slides a hand over to stroke his thumb over me while we ride together.

"Wyatt," I try to say, but the breath is stolen from me

the second I open my mouth. I arch my back and throw my head back, clenching myself on top of him and watching as he starts to go wild beneath me. He pushes himself up into a sitting position and wraps one of his hands around my head, pulling my lips to his feverishly.

He scoots us to the end of the bed slowly and gently, him still inside of me, then stands up, and I'm impressed by his strength. He lays me back down gently, his eyes pouring into mine as he moves in and out of me again, faster, harder, clutching onto me as he does.

As he's moving, he pauses for a minute, and I look up at him.

"What is it?" I ask. He smiles and kisses my calf that's now perched on his shoulder.

"Just thinking," he says between kisses, "it would make this easier tomorrow if you hated me again."

I smile back at him, and I feel those tears pierce my eyes again. I reach up and pull him down to me for one last kiss.

"Never," I whisper then throw myself back on the bed to let him finish taking every piece of me that's left. He holds my hips in the air, and the angle drives me to come faster than I expect. I call out his name one more time as he lowers himself down on me again, letting himself empty everything into me. He slides out of me and collapses next to me then slinks his hands around my arms and pulls me up onto his chest.

After a few minutes, we clean up then make our way back to his bed. I bend to reach for my shirt, but he steps on it. I look up at him.

"Not yet," he whispers, bending down to kiss me gently as he takes my hand and pulls me to his bed. He holds the sheet up, letting me slip in next to him, then pulls it down on top of both of us.

I feel his arms wrap around me as we look out over the city. His face is buried in my hair, and I tighten my grasp on him. We lie in silence for a while, and I think he's asleep, but then he stirs.

"You have to leave soon, huh?" he asks. I close my eyes and swallow back the fear of reality I've been battling since we got back in bed.

I nod slowly.

"Yeah, I should." I'm not sure how to fix this. Because with him, there's a hole in my family. There's a hole in our unit. But without him, there's a hole in me that gets bigger every time I leave. I feel his arms loosen around me in defeat. I turn to face him, tracing his lips with my thumb, kissing his forehead. "But not yet. I want to be yours a little while longer."

He closes his eyes and pulls me in close to him.

"Maryn," he whispers, "you can be mine always."

I blink, and a tear rolls down my cheek, landing on his chest.

26

MAY 2015 - MARYN

D ad lunges forward toward the remote to turn it up. Mom sits on the arm of his chair, and Tucker sits on the couch. I stand in the background.

I'm watching my dad, his eyes glued to the television. He's hanging on every word, every silent moment before the police chief takes his stand at the podium for the press conference.

The words *"Breaking: Found Body Possible Tilden Girl"* keep streaking across the screen in bright red.

The captain makes his way out of the glass door to the precinct, clears his throat, and repositions the microphone.

"Ladies and gentleman, thank you for being here this afternoon," he says. Captain Franks is a tall man with a bit of a pot belly. He's been the Tilden police chief since before I was born. "At approximately 6:30 this morning, Tilden police received a call from Meinhart police regarding a body of an adolescent teenage female discovered in Sheldon Park in Meinhart, 30 miles outside of Tilden lines. The body was discovered in the woods near the jogging path toward the west end of the park. It was transported back to the Tilden station this morning for an autopsy and family identification.

"After testing and a positive I.D., it was concluded that the body discovered was that of Willa Mills, the Tilden resident who went missing in December of last year."

Mom gasps, and Dad brings a hand to his mouth, staring at the screen. I watch as tears form in his eyes, and I feel them doing the same in mine. I'm crying for Willa, and I'm crying for my dad. Because after all he's had to go through over the past few months, he's also dealing with loss. His career made him a man who cares deeply for the students he taught, and now he's suffering through the loss of one—the definitive, infinite loss.

"Her poor parents," Mom says, squeezing Dad's hand. "I can't even imagine."

Tucker turns to us.

"And her brother."

Mom and Dad pause for a moment then nod.

"The whole family," Dad agrees then stands up from his chair and makes his way up to his study and gently closes the door.

Captain Franks is still talking on the television.

"Further testing will be conducted as we do believe there is some DNA evidence present on the body that might bring us to further leads. We will report on that as we have more information. No questions, please. Thank you."

Mom shakes her head and turns the television off, letting us all sit in silence.

. . .

THE NEXT FEW days in school are weird. People are crying in the halls. It's depressing as hell, but the fact that someone killed her—and we still don't know who that someone is—is a bit jarring, too. In homeroom, we get a letter to be brought home to our parents that mentions extra counselors should any of the student body need extra support. Then, details of Willa's funeral arrangements were handed out.

When I get home from school, Dad's making a salad in the kitchen. I walk up behind him and wrap my arms around him, resting my head on his back. He stops pulling the lettuce apart and puts his hands on mine.

"Hey, kid," he says.

"Hi," I say, pushing the handout on the counter in front of him. "They gave this out today at school. I wasn't sure if you'd want to go, but I know Willa meant a lot to you."

Dad stares down at the paper, nodding his head slowly.

"Thanks, kid. All my students mean a lot to me. This one hurts," he says. I squeeze his hand.

"I'll go with you, if you want," I say. He looks up at me and smiles.

"I'm not sure I should go to the actual service, kid. I don't want to cause any raucous. But I do want to visit her after."

I nod.

"I'll come." He smiles and nods then kisses my forehead and continues preparing the salad.

The week passes slowly, and school on Friday is almost completely empty. Half the students and staff are at the funeral, and the other half are pretending to have gone. I'm sitting in chemistry with our substitute and one other kid, scrolling through Facebook on my phone. So many posts, so many pictures of Willa floating around that it makes my stomach hurt.

At the end of the day, my dad pulls up outside of the school to pick me up. He started at the county admin office a few weeks ago, and I can see, every day, more and more of his color has been drained from him.

"Mind if we stop by the cemetery?" he asks as we pull out of the school lot. I wonder how much it tugs at his heart any time he comes here to get me. If he has the urge to park in his old spot, check out his classroom, make sure his kids are keeping up their grades. "The service should be over now."

I nod slowly.

"Sure," I say.

We drive to the outskirts of town and pull into the Tilden Towne Cemetery through the side gate. Dad stops for a moment to look around for the site. When we see the green tarp still laid on the ground, we know we've found hers.

We drive down the driveway a little longer till we reach it. Dad goes to get out of the car but pauses to reach into the backseat. He pulls out a single red rose, takes a breath, then gets out of the car. I get out, too, but I hang back by the car. He needs a minute, I know.

I watch as Dad walks over to the gravesite slowly. He's not speaking out loud, but I know he's saying something. Out of the corner of my eye, I see a figure walking down the hill behind us, then it stops. I look back and see him—Wyatt Mills.

He's still wearing his suit, his tie is undone, his hands in his pockets. He's strikingly handsome, but it's hard to notice because of the disdain I've felt toward him over the last few months. But the sight of him, right now, with his eyes staring straight ahead at my dad, is taking my breath away.

His eyes are narrowed, and I'm waiting for him to speak up, to charge my dad, to tell him to get the hell away from his sister. But he doesn't. Instead, he watches as Dad kneels down to place the rose then walks back to our car.

I don't say anything to my dad about him. I just keep my eyes trained on him. Finally, he flicks his to me, and my breath catches again. We look at each other for a moment; we speak no words; we make no motion.

I hate him. But in this moment, we're at an impasse. The air clears between us as Dad gets in the driver's seat. I look at Wyatt one last time then duck down into the car as we drive away. I see him in my sideview mirror, walking toward his sister's gravesite, all alone, kneeling down in the grass, his hands clasped between his knees.

And for that one moment, I close my eyes and hope that he's not in too much pain.

Just for that one moment.

27

WYATT

When I woke up the next morning, she was already gone. I knew it before I even opened my eyes, because I didn't feel her against me. I felt empty.

When I rolled over, there was a note on the pillow, scribbled on the back of her business card which I'm assuming is the only thing she could find to write on.

I'll miss being yours.

I clutched it to my chest like a fucking five year old, staring up at my ceiling and willing myself to get out of bed and figure out this mess that I call life.

It's been two more weeks, and I'm still trudging through my apartment in nothing but my boxers, drinking milk from the carton like I'm a teenage animal. I've only heard from her once, when she texted me to tell me that she had an inkling the press releases about the gallery were going to drop soon. I'd thanked her for the heads-up, and she'd asked how I was doing. I stared down at my phone, dying to tell her that I wanted her. That despite my quickly draining savings account and morale, I know it all would be better if I could wrap my arms around her and breathe her in.

But I can't tell her that. Because I know she feels something like this, too. And I know having to choose between me and her family is too big of a burden for her to bear, and I won't do that to her. But let me tell you, this whole "if you love them, then let them go" thing is fucking bullshit.

I've applied to a few jobs, but as I scheduled my interviews, the news of the gallery dropped. My name was suddenly everywhere—on the news, online, in my inbox. Two of the jobs dropped their interview offer; another totally ghosted me.

My phone buzzes on the counter.

"Hey, Ma," I say nervously. I haven't come right out and told my family that I am currently unemployed, and more recently, unemployable. It would be a little difficult to explain.

No, I didn't actually have anything to do with it.

Well, I asked them to blame it on me.

For the girl I'm not dating and that I know I can't be with.

Because I still feel guilty for taking her family down all those years ago.

And because I love her. Because I'm a grown-ass man who can't control his emotions. And because I just want her to be happy.

They'd probably be more understanding than I think, but I just haven't been in my right mind to think about it.

"Hi, honey. Look, your father and I just saw the news," she says. I swallow.

"Ah, yeah, Ma. I'm sorry. I've been trying to muster up the courage to tell you guys," I say.

"We talked to Maryn."

My heart rattles against my chest. I swallow a few more times, blinking.

"You...what?"

"She called us a few days ago. She didn't want us to tell you, but of course, you're my child. We had to check in on you. Especially when we saw it broke."

I blink a few hundred more times. She called my parents?

"What did she...what did she say?"

"Everything. She told us how that rat bastard Calloway kid was really at the center of it. And they were going to let her be the fall person for it all. And how you stepped in."

I swallow and nod to myself.

"Yeah," I whisper.

"Oh, honey," she says with what I think is disappointment in her voice. "I'm so proud of you."

Okay, not the turn I was expecting this to take.

"You are?"

"Of course," she says. "You have always been one to do the right thing, even when it's hard. You follow your gut, and I admire you so much for that, sweetie. I'm so sorry your name is going to get smeared by all of this. The world is such an unfair place, baby."

"Yeah, Ma, it is. But she didn't deserve that, either."

"Tell me something, honey. If she wasn't the girl it happened to, would you have…?"

Her voice trails off, and I smile.

"I don't know, Ma. I'd like to think I would. But jeopardizing my whole career path...phew. I guess she means something, huh?"

I hear a soft chuckle on the other end.

"Tell me, honey. Have you spoken to her much?"

I shake my head to myself.

"Not much, Mom. I think it's over. Our history...it's just too cloudy. It would bring a lot of unnecessary pain to her family. I don't want her to have to go through that."

She pauses for a moment.

"Yeah, baby, I know. But remember, sometimes, clouds clear." I smile. I'm not sure if these clouds will. I think these clouds are permanently parked right over our heads.

"Ma?" I say, the heaviness of the impending date starting to weigh on me.

"Yes, baby?"

"What if he gets it?" I ask, my voice breaking as I stare at the date circled in red on the calendar on the side of my fridge.

She pauses again.

"Sometimes clouds clear," she says again. "Let's just hope they clear for us this time."

I nod.

"Okay, Mom. I'll see you tomorrow."

I LIE in bed that night, staring up at my ceiling fan, watching the blades move in circles so fast that they blend together. I remember the first time I heard his name, saw his face. I close my eyes and try to clear it, wipe it away with images of Willa. Of Maryn. Of literally anything or anyone else.

28

JUNE 2015 - WYATT

A few weeks have passed since Willa's funeral. She had a closed casket, but before the viewing started, the funeral home held a private, open-casket viewing for just the family. My mother couldn't stand it; she'd collapsed when it was opened.

Based on the decomposition, or lack thereof, they told us she hadn't been dead that long when they found her. Which disturbs me even more. We could have found her, if it we had just known where to look. We could have saved her. *I* could have saved her.

At the funeral, Dad stood next to mom, grim and gruff, angry disbelief on his face.

But I stared down at her, convinced this body wasn't really her. It looked like Willa, if she'd been dipped in wax that was a few shades darker than her actual skin tone. The makeup was caked thick on her neck to cover up the bruising from the strangulation that killed her.

The strangulation by someone else's hands.

Someone put their hands around my little sister's

neck and squeezed until the life was gone from her body.

I received my degree in the mail, along with a letter of apology from the university for the "unfortunate circumstances" that kept me from the graduation festivities.

It was a nice gesture, I guess.

I've slowly started applying to jobs but with no real gumption to actually land one. I've grown lethargic and lazy since burying my sister. Like nothing else matters much.

But bills still need to be paid. Loans still need to be paid *back*. And life, as hard as it is to imagine, has to go on.

I'm sitting at dinner with my parents, quietly chewing as I stare across the table at the empty seat.

"Any luck with interviews, boy?" Dad asks, his voice still gruff and thick. I shake my head.

"Not yet," I say. I don't have the heart to tell them it's because I've barely sent a single resume out.

"Something will come soon, hon. I know it."

JUST AS WE'RE about to collect our dishes and head to our respective corners of the house, the home phone rings.

Dad looks up slowly then makes his way to it.

"Mills residence," he says. His eyebrows knit together, and I watch as his broad chest begins to heave. "Yes, we're here."

Mom and I stand perfectly still, our eyes trained on him.

"What is it, Ray?" Mom asks, a hand to her chest.

"They have a suspect in custody. Detective Robinson is coming out to the house."

We wait in the living room. The T.V. is on, but none of us are watching it. We're checking our phones, staring at the screens blankly, waiting for his news.

Finally, we hear the car door outside, and we all jump up.

Dad gets the door and shakes Detective Robinson's hand. He leads him in, and we all take our seats again on the couch and chairs.

"Thanks for meeting with me on short notice, guys," he says. Detective Robinson looks tired. This is a big case for him. He's fairly young, and I know this is the first big case he's been the lead on. I like him because I know that, when they had found Willa, he was as crushed as we were. And it wasn't because of the accolades or the press. It was because he was damn good at his job. He wanted to make things right for a grieving family. He has a daughter. He knows.

"So," he says, scooting forward in his chair and clasping his hands between his knees, "we got the DNA evidence back from where we picked up Willa's body. We just recently got a call in about a suspect who was picked up in Connecticut for some odd behavior, following and potentially stalking another teenage girl."

My mom takes my dad's hand, squeezing it tight. He wraps an arm around her. I swallow and lean forward.

"They're going to compare his DNA to what we recovered here. He drives a black Durango, and the back half of his plates match the partial plate we got from the store cameras."

Tears start to stream down my mom's face.

"We don't have the DNA back yet," he says, "but I'm pretty confident he's our guy."

"Jesus Christ," Mom mutters, tilting her head down and pinching her nose in her fingers.

Dad's quiet, just keeps nodding his head like he's taking it all in.

"What's his name?" I ask. All three heads whip to me.

"Excuse me, son?" Robinson asks.

"Who is he? The guy?"

"Sorry, man, but I can't tell you that until it's final," Detective Robinson says. I nod, feeling my fists clench at my sides. I excuse myself and walk out to the backyard.

29

MARYN

I haven't spoken to him in over a week, mostly because I don't know what to say. It's not easy to speak to someone when all you want to do is tell them how much you need them, how much you want to make them happy, but in the same breath, you know it's never going to be possible.

My parents are slowly coming around. When I say slowly, I mean *slowly*. For the first few days, my dad wouldn't speak to me at all. My mother, in an extremely cold and brief phone call, told me he needed space. Finally, when they wouldn't warm back up to me, I showed up on their porch. It's a lot harder to avoid your kid when she's there in the flesh. We had an emotional conversation that resulted in me profusely apologizing and trying to explain myself, and that ultimately ended in them forgiving me once I told them we split up. Tucker is home, and we're having lunch tomorrow, just the four of us.

Things are starting to feel a little more normal now

with them, but it doesn't stop me from thinking about Wyatt on a daily basis.

I miss everything about him. I miss catching him checking me out in the office. Caldell is so different now. I've truly lost all respect for Rex, and it's hard for me to concentrate at work with Wyatt's office empty. I haven't seen Nate one time. It's like they think if they keep him out of my sight, I'll forget everything he did.

But every time I accept a new project, I feel cheap. Every dollar I help this company make, I know how much of it goes right into the pockets of the bastard who cheated his way to get it, and the father who let him. I've started updating my resume. It's time.

Nights and weekends are a lot less exciting, too. Ellie has tried to distract me, but most of her shifts are at night, leaving me to my own torturous thoughts.

A few times, I've found myself thinking about him before I fall asleep, clutching so tightly to my pillow that I thought it was going to explode. But then my brain plays this cruel trick on me where it replaces the breathtaking image of Wyatt with the terrorized, heartbroken faces of my family.

I'm lying in my bed, flicking through the channels, trying to turn my brain off completely. I roll to my side and pull out my birth control from my nightstand drawer when I see my notebook shoved to the back corner. The same notebook I've been making entries in since I was a teenager. I swallow my pill and pull the book out.

As I begin flipping through the entries, I go from wanting to laugh, to wanting to cry, to cringing. God, teenage hormones really are unfair.

But then I get to the entries from that year. The year of Willa.

And as I turn the pages, a clump of folded up newsprint falls from them. I reach down to pick them up and carefully unfold them. And I have the most horrendous case of deja vu I've ever had in my life.

It's like I'm reliving the whole ordeal through a few stupid newspaper clippings. But it all comes rushing back to me again.

TILDEN TEACHER PLACED ON LEAVE AMID MISSING PERSON INVESTIGATION.

Under this headline, there's a photo of my father. The same photo taken for his school identification card. He's smiling. He still had his youth, not the harder exterior he grew.

TILDEN TEACHER CLEARED AS A SUSPECT.

Under this one, the paper used the same photo of Dad but only as an inset. There's a photo of Willa in this one that's much bigger.

TILDEN TEACHER REMOVED FROM TILDEN HIGH.

There's no photo of Dad this time. There are pictures of Willa and the grocery store.

BODY FOUND IDENTIFIED AS MISSING TILDEN TEEN.

I freeze as I unfold this clipping. Because there's something I never noticed before.

There's a huge picture of Willa again, but below it is a picture of the police captain at the press conference where he announced that she had been identified. And behind him, on the steps of the station, is the Mills family. Mr. and Mrs. Mills, him with his arm around her. Next to them is their son—my Wyatt. His head is hung, his hands clasped in front of him. He's completely broken. And to think, at this time, I hated him. I hated him when he needed someone.

There's one last clipping, and I unfold it.

SUSPECT IN MILLS CASE CHARGED.

I remember this day. I remember seeing his face on television after they caught the creep stalking some other teenage girl in another state.

Harvey Rett.

I'll never forget his name. Because after they found him, I found a new target for my hatred. Because of Harvey Rett, my dad lost it all. He lost his passion, his relationships. Because of Harvey Rett, the Mills lost their daughter. Because of Harvey Rett, Wyatt Mills said my dad's name.

Because of Harvey Rett, my dad was officially let go by Tilden County at the end of that school year. And after months of trying to find a job, even applying to school districts more than two hours from home, he had nothing. A metal factory out by the shore was hiring, and my dad got the job. The same damn factory job he will probably have to work until he dies. He got that job just before eviction proceedings were about to take place. Just before our little home was almost snatched out from under us.

Just before I needed to send in my first tuition check for Melladon.

The factory job paid the mortgage but only with Mom getting a job at a local craft store.

Our entire world had flipped.

Harvey Fucking Rett.

As I stare down at his mug shot, his hair disheveled,

his eyes glossed over with a sort of darkness that no therapy could cure, my eyes open wide.

Because Harvey Rett is up for parole.

He's up for parole tomorrow.

I fold the clippings back up and scramble up onto my bed, reaching for my phone.

My hand is shaking as I tap on my dad's number.

"Hey, kid," he says after the phone rings a few times. I clear my throat, my voice shaky.

"Hey, Dad," I say.

"What's goin' on? You ready for lunch tomorrow?"

I swallow the lump that's growing in my throat and try clearing it for the millionth time.

"Yeah, um, about that…"

"Yes?"

"I…I…" My voice trails off. It feels like I can't get any air in. My lungs feel like they're frozen, unable to expand. My heart is racing. In all my life, I have very rarely disappointed my parents. And lately, it feels like I've been doing it a lot. And right now is about to be no different. "I can't go, Dad."

Now, he clears *his* throat.

"And why is that?"

I squeeze my eyes shut as I clutch onto my phone.

"Because, Dad. I have to go to Titers."

There's a pause on the other end.

"Titers…Correctional Facility?"

I swallow again and nod to myself as if he can see me. "Yes."

"For what?"

"Harvey Rett," I whisper, and there's silence again. "Harvey Rett's parole hearing is tomorrow."

I hear Dad clear his throat again.

"I see," he finally says, and I feel my stomach drop.

"I'm sorry, Dad. I'm so sorry. But I have to be there for this," I say. I pause for a moment. "I have to be there for him."

30

WYATT

I'm a pretty confident guy. I've done well in my career—until recently, that is. I'm told I'm pretty good looking, although I try not to let that get to my head. Sure, we all have our insecurities, but overall, I'm pretty self-assured.

But park me in a small room at the correctional facility a few feet from my sister's murderer, and that all goes to shit.

They haven't brought him in yet. I'm sitting between my parents, my knee bouncing up and down, up and down. Mom's squeezing my hand so tight that her rings are making indentations on my fingers.

My dad hasn't said a word; he's just staring blankly ahead at the door where they're going to drag that motherfucker through in just a moment's time. A few people have gathered behind us, including Rett's lawyer, some of my aunts and uncles, and some family friends, all coming to support us. It's crazy, though, how you can be surrounded by people, but in times like this, feel so damn alone.

I hear a sniffle, and I look next to me. Mom's lip is quivering. I squeeze her hand back.

"He's not going to get it, Ma," I whisper. "Don't worry."

She nods and pats my knee.

He won't get it. He can't.

I look down at the folded up piece of paper in my hand. I will be speaking today, essentially begging for Rett to stay where he is until he rots away into nothing. I still find it so sickening that he wakes up every day, breathing in and out, while my sister has been dead for five years. I jotted down a few notes of things I don't want to forget to point out to the judge. I'm looking down at the paper shaking between my fingers when I hear a door open.

My heart stops.

I swallow. I lift my eyes to the door as a guard walks in. I hear the clanking of chains as the guard leads Rett into the room. He looks around but avoids landing his eyes on us. I know he feels us. But he won't look. He's got his scraggly gray hair tied up in a low ponytail. His eyes look black, like endless pits that only see evil. He's wearing a suit today, as if taking him out of his orange jumpsuit makes him look like any less of a criminal.

My chest tightens as he's led to a seat at the front of the room.

A man stands at the front of the room and calls it to order, but suddenly, all I can hear is the blood rushing through my body. I'm trying to focus, but I'm just seeing red. I picture my hands around his neck, squeezing, squeezing, just like he did to my Willa. I picture myself holding on for dear life until his is completely gone.

"I'd like to call up Mr. Wyatt Mills," the man says.

"Brother of Willa Mills." My parents each squeeze one of my hands, and I stand slowly, my legs like gelatin beneath me.

I slowly slide out of the aisle and walk to the front of the room. I stand before the panel in front of me, and my eyes move slowly to Rett. He won't look me in the eye, and it's making me even more mad.

I feel my fists balling at my sides. I'm struggling to take in a deep breath. My head is pounding, and I can't focus my eyes on anything.

If this doesn't work, if the judge doesn't truly *hear* me, Harvey Rett could walk free. Doing what he's done, killing who he's killed, and this bastard could still walk out of the prison.

I grab hold of a podium that's next to me to steady myself.

I'm looking around for a lifeline, anything to bring me back down to earth.

And then I see her.

Maryn Porter. The girl I broke. The girl I put back together. The girl who gave me everything I was missing. Our eyes meet, and she nods, giving me the push I need to go on. I'm still shaky, but she won't take her eyes from mine. And that's all I need.

31
MARYN

I can see him breaking, barely holding it together. I can see him shaking where he stands. I'm not used to this. But when our eyes meet, I feel him take a breath. I can't say it to him out loud, but I'm telling him that, no matter what happens, it's going to be alright. He will get through this. *We* will get through this. Because I'm not sure about the rest, but I know that we have to be a "we."

He's about to begin when the side door to the room opens again. All eyes turn to the door, and my breath whizzes from my lungs when I lay eyes on my father.

He doesn't say anything. He walks down the aisle and slides onto the chair next to me in the back row. He reaches a hand down and squeezes mine, never taking his eyes from the front of the room. And then I see him nod to Wyatt.

Telling him with his eyes that he will get through this.

That *we* will all get through this.

That Willa's death won't be in vain.

I can't believe my father is here. But it's exactly what Wyatt and I both need.

Finally, Wyatt speaks.

"I'm here today to testify on behalf of my sister, Willa," he says. His voice is shaky at first. He clears his throat and goes on. "She would have been twenty-one years old today. But she didn't make it to her sixteenth birthday because of the man in front of you today."

There's this heaviness that comes over the room as everyone around us is listening, hanging on Wyatt's every word.

"She and I were on a quick trip to the grocery store a little over five years ago. She went inside and never made it back out to my car because this man," he says, pointing a finger directly at Harvey Rett, "decided to take her."

Harvey's eyes are wide, but he still won't look at Wyatt. He won't give him that satisfaction.

"Over the course of a few months, detectives with the Tilden Police Force used DNA evidence and a partial license plate to find Mr. Rett, who was, at the time of apprehension, stalking another teenage girl."

My throat feels dry. It's been so long since I've heard all the nitty-gritty details of what happened to Willa. When it was finally revealed what actually *did* happen, I tended to avoid the news stories. Some of it, I didn't want to know.

I'm really glad my dad is here, in this moment, letting me physically and emotionally lean on him.

"My sister was found thirty miles away, in Meinhart, three months after she went missing. After an autopsy, it was determined she died from strangulation."

Wyatt pauses for a moment then lifts his eyes to Harvey Rett.

"Harvey Rett killed my sister with his bare hands. After further examination, it was determined that my sister—" he says, pausing to put his hand to his mouth.

Oh, no. This is the hard part. I remember reading the first few lines of the news reports and then clicking out of the article.

Wyatt collects himself. I hear Mrs. Mills stifling a cry as Mr. Mills stares on.

"It was determined that my sister was also sexually assaulted."

A small gasp goes up in the room. Wyatt's green eyes are wide, full of hate.

I can't stand seeing him this way.

"Harvey Rett took it upon himself that night to take what wasn't his. He decided to prey on an innocent young girl three days before Christmas. He took away her innocence; he killed her without remorse; and then he got right back out into the streets to look for another young woman to prey on. Harvey Rett is a danger to our society, to our daughters, and to the walls of the justice system, if you choose to release him."

The people on the panel all stare at Wyatt, wide-eyed. Man, my man has a way with words.

"If you release him, you're putting your community in danger. You're setting another family up to sit and wait for months, wondering if they will ever see their daughter, their sister, their friend again. If you release him, he will kill again. And when he does, that blood will be on your hands. Thank you."

Wyatt straightens out his tie then walks calmly back over to his family. His mother hugs him, and his father rubs his back. He turns back to look at us. He smiles at me and nods slowly at my father. A few more people step up to speak, most pressing the panel not to even consider parole. Rett has one character witness, an aunt who looks to be pushing ninety, but it almost seems like a struggle for her to say anything nice about him.

Finally, the proceedings end. The room is dismissed, and a decision will be made within twenty-four hours. I let out a long breath. My dad looks over to me and nods.

"Let's have some faith," he says quietly. I pause to see if there's a chance I can talk to Wyatt, but he and his parents are being ushered out, surrounded by the friends who came to support them. As the room begins to clear, Dad and I follow the crowd out the doors.

When we get outside, we're quiet for a moment, walking silently toward the parking lot.

"Dad, I—" I start to say, but he starts to speak, too.

"Kid, I need to say something," he says. We stop walking and turn toward each other. "You were right. About this. About all of it. Holding onto that hate wasn't doing any good for any of us. And in the grand scheme of things, they still lost a child. Wyatt lost a sister. Houses, jobs…we can get those back. But Willa can't be replaced."

I swallow back tears and nod.

"He's a really good guy, Dad," I say with a shy smile. Dad smiles back at me.

"He has to be if you like him," he says, nudging my shoulder. "Well, if you like him, I'd like to meet him—officially," he adds coyly. I smile and nod. I can't think of anything else I'd rather do.

I swallow, thinking about the possibility of Wyatt and me working out. Our families meeting. Going to dinner with my dad. Him and Tucker bonding over sports.

It seemed so out of reach before.

But now that it's not going to make my family implode, I want it more than ever.

"I'll try and set that up," I say with a smile. If it's not too late. If I haven't lost him.

We walk a few more steps, and then I hear his voice.

"Maryn?" he asks, his voice like glass. Dad and I both stop and turn slowly. My heart thuds in my chest. It's crazy what he can do to me.

"Wyatt," I say.

"You're here," he says, his voice hushed. He keeps his eyes trained on me for a moment then turns to my dad. "Mr. Porter. It was so nice of—" he starts to say but is cut off when my dad reaches out and pulls him in for a hug.

"I'm so sorry, Wyatt," I hear him say, and my heart swells. "I'm so sorry for everything your family went through."

Wyatt wraps his arms around my dad tight, and they hold each other for a moment.

"Mr. Porter, I'm sorry too," Wyatt tells him. They pull apart, but Dad keeps his hands on Wyatt's shoulders.

"This will all work out how it should, son," Dad says. "Keep the faith."

Wyatt nods. Dad turns to me.

"Well, kid, I need to get back to the factory. You'll keep me updated?" he asks. I nod.

"Thanks for coming, Dad," I say. He kisses my forehead, shakes Wyatt's hand one more time, then heads to his car.

Wyatt and I walk in silence for a few seconds. Just as we make it to the curb, we hear a voice behind us.

"Wyatt!"

It's Mrs. Mills with Mr. Mills trailing behind her.

"Wyatt!" she cries again.

"Ma? What is it?" he asks. She reaches us and grabs his arms.

"Honey, he's not getting parole," Mrs. Mills says.

"He's…he's not? How do you know?"

"Eduardo. He just heard from the panel. The judge really took your testimony to heart and said that Rett is a danger to the public. He's going right back in."

Mr. Mills comes closer and slaps a hand on Wyatt's back.

"Good job, boy," he says.

I can see the relief settling in on Wyatt almost instantly. I can see his pain. I can see his hope. I can see it all, swirling around above his shoulders now, taking its deadening weight with it.

He hugs both of them.

"Thank God," he whispers as he finally pulls away.

Mrs. Mills lays eyes on me and clears her throat. Wyatt realizes that I'm still standing next to him and does the same.

"Oh, Ma, Pops," he says, putting his hand on the small of my back and nudging me forward, "this is Maryn Porter."

There's an awkward silence for a beat, and then Mr. Mills, who is a handsome, darker version of Wyatt, steps closer to me. He wraps his big arms around me and pulls me in for a long hug.

"It's nice to finally meet you, sweetie," he says. Mrs. Mills takes me in her arms next.

"Yes, we've heard about you," she says with a sweet smile. I blush and smile.

"Thank you both. It's so nice to meet you," I say. We make plans to have dinner with them next week, and then we say our goodbyes.

Wyatt and I walk, hand in hand, weightless together. Since we first met—or, re-met—there have been all these obstacles, all these walls between us, ready to crush whatever possibility there was of "us." But now, they are all gone. There's nothing between us except for the sheer chemistry, attraction, and mutual adoration.

There's nothing between us now except for the understanding that we can take it all, whatever it may be, together, hand in hand, just as we are right now.

"I STILL CAN'T BELIEVE you're here," Wyatt says, looking down at me. I swallow.

"How could I not be?" I ask. "There was no way I was leaving you to do this alone." He smiles at me.

"So, uh, it doesn't sound like your dad hates my guts anymore," he says, his tone more playful now.

"Nope," I say with a smile. "Doesn't sound like it." He takes a step closer to me. There's a cool fall breeze, and it blows my hair all over the place. He lifts his finger to push a piece off my face.

"And you?" he asks with a smile.

"Nope, I don't hate you either," I say. "Actually, I kind of love you." He laughs, and the sound is music to my ears. I take his hands. "Wyatt, he's gonna stay put. I know it."

I can see the worry in his eyes, the fear behind them.

The sadness. But he smiles and nods anyway. He takes my hand.

"I kind of love you, too," he says before he kisses it. "So, what now? I'd say we could go to lunch, but I'm a little tight on cash. I don't know if you heard, but I recently quit my job."

I laugh and pull him in close to me as we start walking.

"Well, I don't know if *you* heard, but I recently got a promotion. So it's my treat," I say, kissing the back of his hand.

32

ONE YEAR LATER - WYATT

"Hi, everyone," I say at the front of the big room. "Thank you all for being here today. I know some of you come from far and wide, so it really means a lot."

It's been a year since I helped keep Harvey Rett behind bars. It's been a year since I resigned from Caldell and really started throwing myself into my foundation work. It's been a year since Maryn was there for me. It's been a year since I made her mine. So as far as years go, this one's been pretty great.

I'm standing in front of the support group I run, which is actually made up of most of the board members of the Willa Foundation.

There are a few families from around the country that we've grown really close to who have all lost a family member to kidnapping or murder. Every meeting, we gain a few more members, and it's harrowing to see the numbers grow.

The mission of our foundation is two-fold. One, we aim to provide support to the family members of the missing person. We can lend an ear, a shoulder, unlike anyone else can. And two, we work with local and national police departments and raise money for rewards, billboard ads, and other avenues to help bring missing people home. In the case that someone's family member has been found deceased, we use raised funds to pay for funerals and legal fees, which is my least favorite part.

But after Willa died, our family went through so much. Emotionally, yes, but also financially, worrying about things that the family of a murdered girl shouldn't have to worry about.

We go around the room introducing ourselves. My parents are chatting in the back of the room with some of the other parents we've come to know. It's a strange connection we have with these people. We all wish we never had to endure the circumstances that brought us here. But we are all so damn grateful to have a small community who understands just what it feels like to have someone literally taken from you.

Today, we're welcoming Jim and Virginia Carlisle. Their four-year-old son, Noah, was kidnapped recently by his uncle, and the two have been missing for over a month. I watch as the other parents greet them, hug them, listen to their stories, offer advice. We're all on this bleak road together, but it makes it a little less bleak to know that we're not alone.

And for the ones who haven't been given a body yet, it gives us a little hope. My Willa might not be coming back, but I like to think she has an eye on Noah.

I look over at Maryn standing at the back of the room. This is the fifth meeting she's been too, and each time, she ends up in tears. I understand. It was like that for me at first. It's a lot to take in. And Maryn, she's one of those people that feels so hard for others. She takes what they're feeling and feels it for them. It's one of the things I love most about her.

I walk over to her as the meeting concludes and wrap my arms around her, leaving a kiss on the side of her head.

"How are you?" I ask her. She gives me a sad smile and wipes a tear from the corner of her eye.

"I don't know how you do this," she says. "It's heart-wrenching. Every single time."

I pull her into my chest.

"I don't know how to *not* do it, ya know?" I ask. She nods.

We clean up after the meeting reception, stack chairs in the event hall that we rent, and pick up some of the trash.

It's nice having her here. She's been such a strong partner with all of this. She's really involved with the foundation, and it makes me fall harder for her every day.

"You ready to go?" she asks, throwing the last few plates and cups in a trash can nearby.

"Almost," I say. "I have to have a quick word with your dad."

Her eyebrow shoots up.

"My dad? Why?"

Mr. Porter has been attending a few of the meetings —I think to show his support for my family since the guns are finally down between us. He's been getting to know the families and offering them an ear. We've found that he's actually really good at leading our meetings, both on the organizational end and on the support side.

I smile and shrug and tell her I'll meet her out front. She kisses my cheek.

"Okay, ya weirdo," she says. As I watch her walk away, I flash back to that moment I watched her walk out of that hotel restaurant a year ago. How she threw that drink on me, that fire in her eyes drawing me in. Sure, things between us there were less than civil then, but the truth is, I wanted her the second I saw her again, and I didn't even realize it then.

I walk toward the back of the room where Mr. Porter is saying goodbye to one of the other board members.

"You ready to head out?" he asks as he sees me approaching. I nod.

"Yep, but before we go, I wanted to talk to you about something," I say. He raises an eyebrow, and I realize in this moment how much Maryn resembles him.

"What's up?" he asks, grabbing two of the chairs beside him and setting them out for us.

"Well, I'm not sure if you heard, but the Willa Foundation was approached recently by the Bell Group. They're the group behind *Find Our Children.*"

Mr. P's eyebrows shoot up again. *Find Our Children* is a national television program run by the parents of a child who was kidnapped in the 90s.

"They have a foundation, too, and they recently reached out to my parents and me to connect, cast a wider net, bundle our resources. They like our therapeutic approach for the families, and they want to invest in getting us some more resources. One of the first things they want to do is hire a few more people full time."

Mr. Porter's eyes widen as he starts to figure out where I'm going with this.

"I'll be coming on as the foundation chair full time. We also need an event leader. My parents and I have been watching you at these last few meetings. We see how naturally you connect with the families, the siblings. I would really like it if you would take the job."

His eyes stay wide as he stares at me.

I know these last few years at the factory haven't been kind to him. I know he has a brilliant mind that's been stifled. I know he has an inherent need to help people, and he hasn't been able to fulfill it.

I also know that he would be the perfect person for the role. These people need him.

"I...I don't know what to say," he says, and I notice his hands trembling.

"Say you'll think about it?" I ask.

He smiles.

"Don't need to. I'd love to work with you all. For these people...and for Willa," he says. I put my hand on his shoulder.

"For Willa," I say. We stand up and fold our chairs up, getting ready to walk back out to the front of the building. But I pause.

"Mr. P.?" I ask.

"Hmm?"

"I need to ask you something else."

"Hit me."

"Not just yet, but a little while from now...would it be okay if I asked Maryn to marry me?" I ask, my voice suddenly shaky.

He stops dead in his tracks and turns to me. It's dead silent for a moment, and then a smile spreads across his face. Before I realize what's happening, he pulls me in for a long, hard hug.

"Absolutely," he says. I squeeze him back.

"Thank you, sir," I say.

"What's this love fest going on in here?" we hear Maryn ask as she makes her way toward us.

I look at Mr. Porter.

"Well, kid, Wyatt here just offered me a full-time position with the foundation," he says, and I breathe a sigh of relief.

Maryn's eyes shoot from her father, to me, back to her father, and back to me. Then, she throws her hands up in the air and squeals.

"What?" she asks. "Oh my...oh, Dad! Oh, Wyatt, I...oh, Dad! No more factory work!"

We both laugh as she gathers herself, wrapping an arm around each of our necks.

LATER THAT NIGHT, Maryn and I are on the couch in my apartment, watching television. She hasn't fully moved in yet, but she basically lives here. Ellie has a pretty serious boyfriend that stays at their place all the time, and apparently, they are less than quiet while having sex. But aside from that, I like to think that Maryn also enjoys being with me.

About six months ago, she got a job with none other than Landry Hotels, right here in New York at one of their satellite offices. She's on their marketing and communications team, and one of the first things she did was terminate their partnership with Caldell Communications and move it to another agency. I'm insanely proud of her. She always said she would have my job one day, but she was wrong. She's going to rule the whole fucking world.

She's lying against my chest, shoveling handfuls of popcorn into her mouth as I stroke her hair. When she's done, she turns to me.

"I can't believe you did that for Dad," she says. I smile and shrug.

"I did it for him...and for you. But I also did it for those people. They need him. Willa would like my choice," I say.

She pushes up on her knees and wraps her arms around my neck. She kisses my jaw, my nose, and then my lips. She smiles.

"I think Willa would like my choice, too."

ACKNOWLEDGMENTS

First and foremost, I have to thank my family. No one will ever know the ups and downs that our little unit has been through, and no one will ever know how much stronger we are because of them. I love you psychos.

This next part sounds sarcastic, but it's truly not. I'd like to acknowledge the people I've come across who spew hate; the people who spread rumors, the "neighbors" who are anything but neighborly. It's because of you that I learned that everything isn't always what it seems, and not to be so quick to judge.

To my blogger team who is constantly, CONSTANTLY waiting and willing to help read, promote, and spread the word about these books, I LOVE YOU and I can't thank you enough. Seriously! I know you get thanked a lot, but I want to take a moment just to tell you how amazing you make the #bookstagram community. From the bottom of my heart, I can't say it enough.

To Will and our babies, thank you for being the reasons why I keep doing what I love, and why I will never stop. Will, thanks for just sitting and letting me listen to the same writing playlist over, and over, and over again, and never judging my song choices (at least out loud).

To my writer friends, thanks for the constant reminder that I can always do more, write more, try more.

ABOUT TAYLOR

Taylor Danae Colbert is a romance and women's fiction author. When she's not chasing her kids or hanging with her husband, she's probably under her favorite blanket, either reading a book or writing one. Taylor lives in Maryland, where she was born and raised. For more information, visit www.taylordanaecolbert.com.

Follow Taylor on Instagram and Twitter, @taydanaewrites, and on Facebook, Author Taylor Danae Colbert, for information on upcoming books!

Are you a blogger or a reader who wants in on some secret stuff? Sign up for my newsletter, and join **TDC's VIPs** - Taylor's reader group on Facebook for exclusive information on her next books, early cover reveals, giveaways, and more!

OTHER BOOKS BY TAYLOR:

IT GOES WITHOUT SAYING

BUMPS ALONG THE WAY

OFF THE RECORD

ROWAN REVIVED

NOTE FROM THE AUTHOR

Dear Reader,

I can't tell you what it means that you've decided, out of all of the books in all the world, to read mine.

If you enjoyed reading it as much as I enjoyed writing it, please consider leaving an Amazon or GoodReads review (or both!). Reviews are crucial to a book's success, and I can't thank you enough for leaving one (or a few!)!

Thank you for taking the time to read FIGHTING WORDS.

Always,
TDC
www.taylordanaecolbert.com
@taydanaewrites

Made in the USA
Middletown, DE
21 February 2020